Passionate Desire

Bad boy businessman Joe Bradshaw has almost everything he wants in life, except for his straight-laced colleague Victoria Collins. She is proving to be an elusive challenge. When a stalled elevator locks them together, he takes a chance and discovers the sensual woman beneath the drab exterior. Once he's had a taste of her, Joe is determined to break through Vicki's barriers to free the erotic woman hiding inside.

Victoria may have given into her powerful attraction to Joe Bradshaw in the elevator, but she has to keep a grip on her impulses going forward. She is stalked by her past – her ex-fiancé will stop at nothing to get her back. She's worked hard to stay safe, and needs to stick to her plan.

As Vicki resists surrender, can Joe get her to trust him to safeguard her heart?

Passionate Desire

MARIE TUHART

Published in the United States of America First Printing: 2017

Print book

ISBN -13: 978-1-943407-23-1

Trifecta Publishing House

1120 East 6th Street

Port Angeles, Washington 98362

TRIFECTA PUBLISHING HOUSE

Contact Information: Info@TrifectaPublishingHouse.com

Editor: Elizabeth Jewell

Cover Art by Designed by Diana

Formatted by CyberWitch Press

DEAR READER,

This book was originally published in 2010 under the title: In Plain Sight. Since then, I've revised the book and added more than 12,000 words to it. I was able to expand on Joe and Vicki's courtship and showing how they fell in love.

Sincerely,
Marie Tuhart

Chapter One

Victoria Collins glared at the illuminated display panel in the elevator and vowed to kill the entire maintenance department. She could see the headlines now—*Elevator Homicide. TechTronics employee kills because of slow cab.*

She couldn't blame her impatience on having a stud waiting at home. All she had to look forward to was a glass of wine, a hot bath, and her vibrator. But anything beat being in this slug of an elevator alone.

She tapped her foot. The display dragged past the floors. She was only at twenty. Would the day from hell ever end?

First, some ass had run into her, making her spill her coffee down her jacket. Second, her assistant had called in sick. Third, her marketing report had never made it from her department to the vice president's office. Three irritating annoyances.

Tonight she had stayed late to update the report to perfection and carried it up herself, not trusting her report wouldn't be lost again. The display flashed eighteen. The seventeenth floor was next— Joe's floor.

Her nipples hardened behind her lacy bra. She'd had little control over her reactions since he had come to work at the company several months ago. Oh, yes, her breath caught in her throat. Joe had bad-boy written all over him. He was handsome, with a work ethic that rivaled her own. Victoria held her breath as seventeen lit up and stayed solid. The elevator shuddered to a stop.

Could it be him? *Oh, get a life, Victoria.* Why would he, the company's newest wonder boy, be working late on a Friday night? He was no doubt out partying with any number of gorgeous women in downtown Seattle. Probably some other poor sap working late tonight.

She kept her attention on the display when the doors opened, wishing the person would hurry up and board the elevator so they could get on their way.

The spicy scent of pure male and citrus surrounded her. Oh, dear Lord. She knew the scent—it turned her bones to water every time. Only *he* smelled like that. She closed her eyes in a brief moment of ecstasy before the doors slid shut, reminding her of where she was. Alone in the elevator—well, not now.

Her gaze connected with his. Clear blue eyes danced with delight. His black hair was long enough to cause the ends to curl in a sexy way at his collar. His tailored gray jacket covered his broad shoulders, the tie a shade lighter, contrasting with his white shirt. His hands in the pockets of his dark slacks pulled the fabric tight over his hard thighs and ...

She swallowed, forcing her gaze away from his incredible body. He was watching her. Shit. "Good evening." Oh, Lord, was that her breathy, soft voice?

"It is now," he said, and a slow smile tugged his lips. His voice was husky with the right amount of sex appeal, and his smile ... She gulped. The smile reminded her of a predator who had cornered its prey so they could play sensual games.

He's just a man.

Oh, yeah, but what a man. Moisture dampened her panties.

Damn, she didn't want to be attracted to him, to lust after him.

A loud bang startled her out of her thoughts. The elevator jerked to a stop, throwing her off balance—and straight into Joe Bradshaw's arms.

"Are you okay?" His fresh minty breath brushed her cheek.

The warmth of his fingers curled around her arms sent shivers of awareness and arousal singing through her veins. "I'm fine." She forced herself to keep her voice steady and calm, even though her heart raced like an out-of-control freight train. She extracted herself from his hold even as she longed to stay in his embrace. "What happened?"

"The elevator stopped." There was no mistaking the amusement in his voice as he stepped to the control panel. He pressed his long, tapered finger against the emergency button.

Nothing happened.

He shot her a glance, brow raised, then turned back, opened the small metal door, and lifted up the phone.

How would those fingers feel on her skin? Against her breasts, caressing her nipples, in her pussy? *Oh, God!* If she didn't stop this, she'd climax without him even touching her. And she couldn't do that, it would reveal too much.

After several moments, with precise, almost delicate care, he replaced the receiver. He faced her with a wicked light burning in his eyes. "The guard's not answering the phone. He must be on his rounds. I pressed the emergency button, but there's no response. We may be stuck here for a while. These elevators haven't been upgraded with cameras yet." His tone was bland, but the speech flowed through the unmistakable curve of a smile, as if he were happy they were trapped here. He couldn't want to be stuck with her, could he?

Her pulse quickened. "We can't be stuck." No, no, no. Not today, not with him. *Oh, please, please.* Anxiety swept through her.

How could she hide her arousal if they were trapped together in this damn elevator? Could he smell the musky scent? With weak knees, she wobbled over to the buttons and pressed. Nothing.

Fumbling with the zipper on her purse, at last she got it open and pulled out her cell phone. 'No service' flashed. She shoved it back. Shit. She was stuck in the elevator with a man who oozed sex. Of course, having spent the last six months fantasizing about him day and night didn't help ease her frustration. She leaned against the elevator wall, trying to keep some space between them.

Why not take advantage of the situation? Could she? No, she couldn't. After she had been fired for her last workplace romance, she had decided never to mix business and pleasure again. The price was too high. But the Fates had seen fit to put temptation in front of her. The pros and cons weighed in her mind. She didn't report to Joe, so that was a plus. Yet they worked for the same company, and others might see them together, a minus. A plus, she was attracted to him. A minus, she was in lust with him. Oh, damn, her head was spinning. How could she fight herself, Joe, and temptation?

"Are you claustrophobic?" he asked, as he stood a few feet from her. He appeared totally relaxed except for those intense blue eyes watching her.

"No, but … " Her mouth became dry as the Sahara, and all coherent speech escaped her when he shrugged out of his jacket. His white shirt molded tight across his shoulders, showing off his muscular chest.

"Good. Tell me why you've been avoiding me." His husky tone sent shock waves through her body.

Her eyes widened, and what little bit of breath still in her lungs whooshed out.

HE MIGHT AS well get comfortable, since they'd be here a while.

Joe was very conscious of the complication a workplace romance would create, and he'd held himself back until now. But being thrown together in this elevator, he'd be damned if he was going to let the opportunity pass.

At thirty-four he'd had his share of women, but no woman had fascinated him as Victoria did. He'd been intrigued the moment he had caught sight of her on his first day. A woman who tried to hide her sensuality instead of flaunting it was a woman he couldn't help but notice.

She had a quiet demeanor, but he'd seen the fire in her eyes when someone challenged her in a meeting. He wanted to put that fire there, in a more intimate way.

Right now, though, exhaustion was written on her face. Hell, she'd had this tired look all week. How could anyone miss the slight smudges beneath her beautiful green eyes? Those beautiful sea-green eyes had grown dimmer and more remote as the week progressed. He didn't like how hard she was working.

She had an air of vulnerability around her, and for a moment he almost backed away. But he couldn't resist the temptation to uncover the sensual woman hiding underneath those dowdy clothes. Maybe a nice hot bath and a massage, then they could get on to other intimate pursuits. Other men seemed to miss her soft sexiness. But he didn't. Over the last few months, he'd seen the way she'd glance at him, then away, when he looked at her. When he turned his attention elsewhere, she'd focus in on him again.

Last week she'd ducked into an empty cubicle to avoid him. The thought almost made him smile—almost. But he'd also noted her rapid breathing, dilated pupils, and pebbled nipples whenever they happened to meet. This was the best sign he'd had to date. She was just as affected as he was by the attraction. Now he had the chance, maybe he could find out what made her tick.

He had to make a move. A preemptive strike. If he waited

until she was at top speed, she'd shut him down quicker than a cold shower. He'd seen her do it with other co-workers who flirted with her.

"Got a hot date tonight?" he asked, continuing to stare at her while he draped his jacket over the faux-wood bar at the rear of the elevator.

"No, but I'm sure you do," she blurted.

He arched a black eyebrow, and her cheeks grew warm. Why the heck did she blurt that out to him? Where was her sense of self-preservation? It had disappeared into the stratosphere the second he'd stepped into the elevator.

"Forget what I just said." She pressed her fingers against her forehead. This wasn't her day.

"I'll let it go. Tell me why you're in such a hurry."

"Listen, the only date I have is with a hot bath." How could he appear so fresh after working all day? She knew he'd been in early this morning because one of the secretaries had commented on his sending down several massive reports for typing. He looked so good, it wasn't fair. She tucked behind her ear several wisps of hair that had escaped the twist she wore.

His steady gaze traveled over her body and burned through her clothing. "Hmmm, if we get out of here soon, I'd be interested in sharing." He stepped forward, his breath fanning her cheek.

"What?" She'd lost track of what they'd been talking about. When had he moved closer? She angled her body away from his. "Sharing what?" His heat called out to her, making her want nothing more than to surrender to it.

"Your bath, Vicki." His index finger touched her skin and trailed across her cheek, leaving a path of fire and awareness.

He was touching her. Her mind whirled. Was she dreaming? God, she hoped not. It would be too cruel to wake up and find this had been a fantasy. Part of her wanted to sink into his warmth, the other part warned her this could end in disaster. "You know my name?" She could have slapped herself for asking such a stupid question. Her palms tingled with the need to place them on his chest and feel the solid beat of his heart.

"Yes." His fingers teased her lips before taking a path over her neck to the base of her throat and down to the vee of her jacket.

What was he doing? He'd never seemed interested in her before. Well, it wasn't like he had anything else to do while they were stuck here. She should be insulted. But she wasn't, and she didn't have a clue as to why. Unable to help herself, she closed her eyes, luxuriating in the roughness of the pad of his finger against her soft skin. Her body craved the sensations, reveled in them, even while her brain protested. *This is someone you work with.*

"I know a great deal about you," he whispered, his breath caressing her ear.

She lifted her lashes to gaze at the fine dark stubble on his chin. "Wh … what do you know about me?" *Step away*, her brain ordered. But her legs wouldn't cooperate. Her heart beat so hard she thought it would burst out of her chest at any second.

"I know you're a beautiful woman." His palms cradled her hips. "And you're sexy as hell."

"Sexy?" She gave a harsh laugh. There was nothing sexy about the plain black suit she wore, or the modest heeled shoes, or her hair pulled into a twist and the bare minimum of makeup.

But the woman underneath … well, no one knew about her. How could he have seen through her protective façade? Her insides shook at the thought of Joe getting beneath her carefully built wall.

Joe's hands at her waist held her captive. Why was he touching her? His grip was gentle, almost as if he were afraid of frightening her. She wasn't scared of him physically. Mentally, however, was another matter.

"Yes. Sexy." His blue eyes clashed with hers. "Oh, you've gone to great pains to hide it, but it's still there, especially in the way you move." He shifted closer.

"Mr. … " Her hands fluttered to his chest, intending to push him away, but the second she encountered his warmth she was reluctant to leave it.

"It's Joe, Vicki." He slid closer to her and dipped his head.

"It's Victoria," she said in a firm voice. He'd called her Vicki a second time. No one called her Vicki. Not her parents, not her grandmother. Her heart clenched. Her parents had divorced and remarried so many times she barely talked to them. Her grandmother … a smile crossed her lips. Her grandmother refused to shorten her name. Her stomach clenched with the reminder her grandmother was gone now. With a quick shake of her head, she forced away her memories. Now was not the time.

She should be annoyed with Joe for shortening her name, but instead her insides melted. She angled her head away from his seductive presence, but it didn't help. She could still smell him and feel him—and damn it, she wanted him.

"Vicki is much sexier, and you're one sexy woman."

"Yeah, right." Her spine stiffened. *Enough! Push him away.* But her body wouldn't cooperate. This was crazy. They were stuck together, and he just needed something—someone—to pass the time. She wasn't important to him. And that stung.

"Why do you doubt it?" His palms skimmed up arms and settled on her shoulders. Within the next minute, his hands were in her hair. Seconds later, her blonde tresses tumbled around her shoulders. "Better?" he asked.

"No. It isn't." She managed to get her body to obey and take a step back. She held out her hand. "I'd like my clip, please." He had no idea how precious the gift was to her.

He admired the silver design before slipping it into his pants pocket.

"Mr. Bradshaw, this is very unethical." She fought to keep her tone stern, even though her spine wanted to melt and her lips tingled with the need to kiss him.

"It's Joe."

Victoria shook her head, her hair cascading further. "I can file sexual harassment charges." Her tone was firm.

"But you won't." A grin teased his lips, and excitement raced up her spine. That grin was wicked, sexy, and wildly devilish. She'd never met a man like him.

"What makes you think so?" She didn't like the way he thought he knew what she'd do. Let alone thought of her as a piece of tail. Oh, hell, who was she kidding — they'd been dancing around each other since day one. He was an object of her lust.

"Because this isn't about your job with TechTronics or anything connected with work. This is between you and me."

Shock and disbelief at his presumption had her saying, "There is no you and me." She'd like nothing more than Joe and her. What else had she fantasized about? But she had to stay in control here. She was no longer a man's little puppet. She had shed that persona when she walked out on Derek.

"There will be." His fingers caressed her neck, before cradling her head. He leaned down to capture her lips with his.

She stiffened. This wasn't a good idea. But her body didn't listen. She melted against him and vaguely heard the thud of her purse as it hit the floor before she entwined her arms around his neck.

A part of her wanted this kiss, wanted to be in his arms. She'd wanted this since the first day she'd seen him. After work, she'd spotted him in the lobby of the building looking sexy in jeans and a black leather jacket with a motorcycle helmet tucked under one arm. She was a sucker for the bad-boy look. Now the bad boy was in the elevator with her, taking what he wanted, and she was giving it to him. Brain and common sense be damned.

Her lips parted. The rough texture of his tongue danced over the roof of her mouth before tangling with hers, drawing, pulling it into his own. She tasted mint; he must have brushed his teeth before leaving his office. Odd thought, as their tongues tangled and fought to take control.

When the kiss ended, their harsh breathing filled the silence. She gasped.

"You taste like sin." His voice was deep.

"And how does sin taste?" she asked, surprising herself with her boldness. Inhaling, she tried to get some oxygen to her brain, then maybe she could clear this sensual haze clouding her judgment.

"Delightful. Sweet. Erotic." He nibbled her earlobe. "Do you know what I want to do to you?"

"You want to have sex with me." She gulped. Where was her indignation that he dared to kiss her? Where was her outrage because this could cost her her job? She tried to summon up some anger, but her body didn't care. She was aroused, and damn it, she'd imagined this moment too many times while alone in bed.

"More than sex." His breath caressed her ear before his tongue rimmed it. "I'll touch and lick every inch of your body. When I've made you come from my fingers and my tongue, I'll plunge my cock into your sweet, wet pussy to feel you squeeze and milk me." His gaze drilled into hers as he paused for a moment. "Then we can experiment to see how far over the edge we can drive each other."

Her knees almost buckled. It wasn't fair—she was twenty-eight years old and her body was reacting like Joe was her first lover. Then again, no one had ever had the nerve to talk to her like he did. Not in bed and not alone in an elevator. And damn if just listening to him didn't make her blood burn and her sex tighten.

"Mr. … ah, Joe," she corrected herself, when those blue eyes snapped to her face. "An elevator isn't the place for this type of conversation."

"Why not?" He brought his right hand up between their bodies, toying with a button on her blazer.

"The elevator could start at any second and … " She stopped breathing as he undid the first button, then the second. Even with the material between their skin, his body heat blazed, bore into her skin. Her nipples pebbled even more, begging for his attention.

"I knew it," he whispered with a hint of victory in his voice. He'd uncovered the red lace camisole she wore beneath her jacket. He trailed his index finger over the slopes of her breasts, then he paused. She looked up. "Say you don't want this. Say no and I'll stop."

The struggle on his face was evident, yet she wanted him, and he wanted her, even if it was only for a brief moment in the elevator. "I want this," she whispered, giving him consent and arching into his touch. She wanted him to continue. Forbidden sex in an elevator with a passionate bad boy was a private fantasy come to life, and God help her, she was going to throw caution to the wind and take full advantage of it. Her body demanded it.

And what if you get fired? Her logical side was still alive and working. This could only be one time. No relationship. A relationship would get her fired; one-time sex that no one but the two of them knew about … she should be safe. Unless they were caught.

"Thank God," he rasped as he pushed her blazer off her body.

Her mouth opened but any protest died on her lips as he palmed her breast. Heat enveloped her. He massaged her breast, making it swell, before catching the nipple between his thumb and forefinger and squeezing gently. Her knees gave way and he snagged her around the waist. Hauling her up against his body, he brought her hips into sharp alignment with his. His hardening cock pressed against her core. Her pussy wept in anticipation.

No man had ever aroused her so fast or with such expertise. Her brain was shutting down. The realization the elevator could start and they could be discovered only added to her excitement. Danger heightened her arousal. She grew wetter, moisture soaking her panties as she grew impatient for his cock deep within her.

He tugged her nipple once again before lowering his mouth to it.

Oh, dear Lord. Hot, wet heat surrounded her nipple, spreading out like wildfire. Her head fell back. Her nails dug into the soft flesh of her palms as she curled her hands into fists at her sides. All the while he licked and suckled her through the camisole. Tiny electrical shocks surged through her body straight to her pussy, making it throb with need.

Wet silk clung to her breasts when he lifted his head to stare down at her. "I've wanted to do this since the first day I saw you." His voice was hoarse and his eyes filled with passion as he stared at her.

"What? Getting stuck in an elevator together?"

His husky laugh sent waves of awareness through her veins. "Not the elevator, but tasting you, touching you, fucking you."

His words danced along her nerve endings, causing her stomach to clench with desire. Why had he chosen to make a move on her now? Was it just her availability, her proximity? Her mind tried to reason, but couldn't. Her body's need to devour him, inch by inch, was too overwhelming. When long, male fingers lowered the straps of her camisole, she drew in a startled breath. Cool air touched her skin and her nipples tightened further.

"These are fantastic." His voice was husky with need.

Her head rested against the elevator wall and his lips closed over her naked breast. His tongue licked a path to her nipple, swirled around before he pulled it deep into his mouth and sucked. She arched her back, giving herself to him. Her breasts were sensitive, always had been, but his lips, tongue, and teeth took her to another level. She was burning up. Her stomach tightened as flutters spread from her breasts to her clit and back again. A climax was building.

He nipped lightly, and as her hips surged to meet his, molten hot lust rushed through her. She was ready. Now!

"Joe," she whispered.

An audible *pop!* filled the elevator as he released her nipple. "I've always been a leg man, but your breasts have converted me." His lips kissed a path up to the hollow of her throat, then his tongue dipped into the small depression before tasting his way back to her mouth.

This kiss was hot, hard, and demanding. She didn't even think about resisting. She didn't want to resist. Who was she to throw this chance away? She'd worry about her future tomorrow and even the next day. Right now she wanted this man. She played with his tongue in his mouth, coaxing it to follow hers into her mouth, where they tangled together. He groaned, and a thrill of excitement weaved its way up her spine.

She hadn't expected this. Never in a million years would she have thought she'd melt in his arms this way. Oh, she might have fantasized about him, but never this. Reality was much better. Just for once, she wanted to feel this man's desire for her and only her. Even if it only lasted these few minutes. She wanted Joe, here and now. His hard cock pressed against her core, ready and waiting. She wasn't going to turn back now.

When he lifted his head, she forced her eyes open. His gaze blazed with passion, the fire within the depths burning a path straight to her soul. His palms rested on her stomach, fingers bit by bit inching up the fabric of her skirt. She could hardly breathe. One more touch and she'd go up in flames. But she didn't care, and she wasn't about to let him have all the fun.

Forcing her arms into action, she began to unbutton his shirt and tugged it from his trousers. God, the coarse hair covering his chest was delicious beneath her fingers. She raked her nails across his nipples in a light touch. His quick intake of breath told her he liked it. Her ex had hated anything near his nipples. "I want to taste you," she said, her pussy clenching with need.

"Go ahead." Desire and need filled his voice. "I want you to."

A sense of power wrapped her in its intoxicating spell. Lowering her head, she licked him, her tongue darting in and out like a cat. He tasted salty and masculine. Pure delight flowed through her body at his groan of pleasure. The sound was more than enough encouragement. She laved one hard nub then the other while her fingers trailed over his lower back, where the play of muscle beneath her palms delighted her senses.

He cupped her jaw, lifting her mouth to his. Another demanding kiss, their breaths mingling in the heat of passion. He pushed her against the elevator wall; his erection throbbed. She wormed her palm between their bodies and brazenly cupped him.

A shudder swept through his body and he broke their kiss. "Take out my cock." His demanding tone was thick with desire.

For a second her heart stopped beating, then with great care she lowered the zipper, found the opening in his briefs, and brushed her fingers across his smooth hardness. His penis jumped, short-circuiting any rational thoughts she had left. Pushing his shorts down, she encircled his thick shaft and his hips shifted forward, pressing into her palm.

He was so thick. And so long. The veins of his cock stood out and the head glistened. She ran her fingers over it, spreading his wetness. Thinking about his length surging into her had her biting her lower lip to contain her excitement.

"My turn." His tone was playful and deep.

He plucked at her zipper and the back of her skirt gave way, then his palms slid down to her hips, pushing the fabric down until it fell at her feet. Cool air caressed her legs. "Please." The pleading tone in her voice surprised her. "Soon," he whispered as his hands landed on her thighs. "Garters." He all but groaned out the word. "God, woman, you're sex on two legs."

Her breath caught in her throat when he cupped her through her panties. Automatically, her legs widened. She was so hot, so wet. Her sex throbbed for his touch and his cock.

She didn't have to wait long. With a hard tug, he tore her panties from her and slid a finger between her slick, wet folds. Unable to help herself, she pushed her pelvis forward and widened her stance even more. He slipped in a second finger, and she groaned. God, it felt so good. So damn good.

She kept stroking his cock, feeling his need, his heat, his hardness, wanting all he could give her and more.

"I can't wait," he muttered. "I've got a condom in my back pocket."

With trembling fingers, she found the small foil packet. Somehow she managed to open it, rolling it down his pulsing cock. "Done."

The word had just left her lips when he lifted her. "Put your arms around my neck, then wrap your legs around my waist," he ordered, his voice tight.

There was no hesitation. She did as he demanded. She wanted this. No, *needed* this. At the touch of his cock at her entrance, her breath whooshed out. His fingers had stretched her, but he seemed impossibly big.

Anchoring her against the wall, he bent his knees, then thrust up.

"Ah!" The sound was torn from her throat as he penetrated her. God, he was enormous. She struggled to find not only her voice but also her breath. "Too big," she gasped.

"It's okay, baby," he whispered, hot and ragged against her ear. He stilled, waiting for her to adjust to him. Then, as her inner muscles relaxed, he pushed in another inch.

She panted. His cock slowly filled her, and she felt every vein. Pure pleasure flowed through her body. This time she couldn't help but grind her hips into his, wanting more of him. All of him.

"You're so damn tight." His breathing grew more erratic.

"It's been a while." Her heart pounded and she couldn't catch her breath. If she were to die right now, it would be in pleasure. Her head bumped the wall when he thrust deeper into her. "Stop," she begged.

He became motionless in response to her plea. His muscles quivered beneath her palms, but she feared she couldn't accommodate him in this position. He was too large, too hard, and too damn male. "So hot, so wet, so tight," he said, burying his face in the curve of her neck and licking her skin.

She wanted him, but fear hit her. He was tightly embedded inside her, straining her to the limit, and she was pretty sure she couldn't take any more, no matter how much she wanted to. A tremor shook her body. "I need just a minute." She took a deep breath and let it out. "I'm okay, now."

"Easy. I'll take it slow. Later you can take all of me into your sweet, blazing pussy," he whispered against her skin before withdrawing and sliding back in. With slow and gentle movements, he stroked her. Her garters strained with every move.

His body rocked against hers, easing himself in and out with measured thrusts. Fear began to dissipate as her body opened more and more to him. Filling her with his cock, he made her want even more. She was amazed when her hips began to undulate, pressing down as he thrust up. Sensations built, like a fire fed a little at a time until it blazed into full glory. Her muscles clenched around his thick cock and the tingling in her belly erupted out of control.

She was going to explode. "Joe." Victoria whispered his name as the tremors increased.

He took her mouth a second before the trembling overwhelmed her and she screamed out her climax. When he released her, she gasped for air. Her pussy continued to flex around him, wanting more, until she came down from the sensual haze of satisfaction.

"You … ahh … you're still hard." It was difficult to get the words out. He pulsed inside her, fueling her desire to take him again.

"Doesn't matter." He lifted her until his cock sprang free, then set her on her feet, holding her by the waist until she could stand without assistance.

The strain was etched on his face and his wrinkled forehead. He was denying himself pleasure to make sure she got hers. Her heart warmed.

"But it matters to me." With a sense of bravado she didn't know she possessed, she dropped to her knees. She removed the condom from his throbbing shaft, dangling it between her fingers as her free hand caressed him.

"Vicki," he groaned.

She smiled, petting the head of his cock before taking him into her mouth. She dropped the condom onto the floor. God, he was huge. No wonder he'd stretched her body to its limit. She couldn't fit all of him in her mouth, but she'd do her best to please him. Placing her fingers around the base, she stroked his cock as she sucked and licked. His musky scent overpowered the lube of the condom. Her own desire flared, and a sense of power cascaded through her. She did this to him. She made him stiff and wanting.

His fingers tangled in her hair as she pleasured him. She cupped his balls with her free hand. They were rigid, swollen and drawn up tight against his body. Widening her lips further, she took him deeper into her mouth, and she stroked harder and faster. "Yes," he cried out, his grip tightening. "Baby, I'm going to come."

She didn't pull away; didn't want to. Instead she increased the sucking motion.

With a groan and a slight jerk of his hips, Joe's essence filled her mouth. Tart saltiness lingered on her tongue , but she liked it, and it gave her a deep sense of satisfaction as she swallowed. She'd made him climax.

As his cock shrank, she swirled her tongue around its head. He urged her away, pulling her up from his feet. When she was standing again, he captured her face between his palms and kissed her. He lifted his head, his eyes still burning with passion. "I never expected you to go down on me."

Her face grew warm but she kept her gaze locked with his. "Only fair for me to give you as much pleasure as you gave me." Besides, she'd fantasized about taking him in her mouth. The reality was better than she had imagined.

A ringing sound made them both jump. It was a couple of seconds before either of them realized it was the elevator phone.

Swearing in a low voice, he turned to snatch up the receiver. "Yes." He glanced over at her, the heat from his gaze on her body making her want him again. "I see," he said. "That's fine. Thank you." He hung up. His expression held appreciation as he took in her disheveled appearance. "The guard. He'll have us out of here in a few minutes." He tucked his cock into his pants, rearranging its fit before pulling up the zipper.

"Shit." She reached for her skirt, stumbling as she tried to get it on.

"Easy." He curved his fingers around her waist. "Let me help you." Taking the skirt from her, he knelt. "Brace your hand against the wall."

She did as he suggested. He lifted one of her feet, slipped the skirt underneath, then did the same with the other foot, taking care the fabric didn't get caught on her shoes. When he pulled the skirt up her body, his fingers brushed against her calves, then her thighs and her hips before settling at her waist. As he stood, his chest rubbed her sensitive breasts as he reached around her, tugging up the zipper on her skirt. A sigh escaped her when he stepped back.

He bent over then straightened. "Sorry I can't help you with your panties, they're useless." He held up the torn fabric before slipping them into his pants pocket. His eyes twinkled, and she knew he didn't regret ripping them from her body.

"I think I'll survive." Tugging the camisole over her breasts, she glanced down. She could still see the bulge in his pants where his cock rested, then the bulge moved. Her gaze snapped up to his face. His teeth were gritted. Was he angry?

"Keep staring at me and everyone will know just how hard I am for you. And trust me, I have very little control where you're concerned. I may have waited a while to make a move, but don't tempt me to take you again in this elevator, rescue be damned."

A husky laugh escaped her lips as she buttoned her jacket. "Maybe I don't want to be rescued." Where the hell were those words coming from?

"Witch." He snagged her around the waist, kissing her until the elevator began to descend.

Once again, Joe knelt. Using his handkerchief, he picked up the used condom and tucked it into his pocket. Then he retrieved her purse and held it out.

Taking it, she forced herself to glance away from his magnetic eyes. She knew her lips were swollen from his kisses. Her breasts were still tender from his touch, and her sex still throbbed with heat. She wanted him again. But she fought the feelings. What was he thinking? Her emotions were tangled into one big knot. She watched him out of the corner of her eye. What did he think of her? His face gave nothing away. He slipped on his jacket just before the elevator pinged and the doors opened.

The guard stood there in his brown uniform, a concerned frown on his face. "Sorry I took so long. I was on my rounds and just heard the alarm a few minutes ago."

"No problem," said Joe, his voice steady.

"Ma'am?" The guard was staring at her. He was doubtless noting her flushed cheeks and the disarray of her hair. Inhaling, she forced herself to exit the elevator, ignoring the way her naked sex tingled beneath her skirt.

"As Mr. Bradshaw said, no problem." Her hair cascaded forward and she pushed it back with an impatient hand.

"Maintenance should check the elevator out. I would hate for anyone else to get stuck," said Joe. He shot her a meaningful look, one she chose to ignore.

"I'll get right on it. Do you need someone to walk you to your car, miss?"

"No, I'll be fine."

The guard looked at Joe.

"Don't worry, I'll take care of Miss Collins."

The guard nodded and took off down the hallway.

"Very good care," Joe whispered in her ear.

Chapter Two

*J*oe slipped an arm around Vicki's waist, cradling her body close to his. He couldn't forget her soft moans of pleasure or how she'd exploded. His cock twitched. Her cheeks were full of color Was she embarrassed? Given what had just happened between them, he hoped not.

During casual conversation with co-workers, he'd learned she kept to herself most of the time, only occasionally joining a small group at Ed's Saloon. When he asked if Vicki was seeing anyone, the answer was always the same. Not that anyone knew of, and if he was intending to pursue her, he'd need body armor.

Many of the guys had joked about how she froze them all out, never taking them up on a drink or a little bit of fun. And now he had an inkling of why she did it. She voiced worry about sexual harassment, so if he had to venture a guess, Vicki had probably been harassed in a job or two. He wouldn't do that, and if she told him to back off, he would.

But he had known there was more below the surface. One had to be willing to peel back the layers of prim Victoria to get to the explosive Vicki. And he was just the man to do it. Of course, he hadn't meant to take her for the first time in an elevator, but when the opportunity had presented itself, he'd pounced. And now he wanted more. He only had to convince her.

"Where's your car?" he asked as they stepped out into the crisp Seattle night, a hint of rain in the cool evening air.

"Mr. Bradshaw." She turned toward him, back straight and hands at her sides, her lips pressed together almost as if she were angry. "I think this is where we say goodbye."

Damn. Victoria was back in control, having shoved aside her sexual urges. Well, he wasn't about to let her escape, not after tasting her sweet nectar. She hadn't said no or to leave her alone. His eyebrows rose, and he crossed his arms while he stared at her. "What are you afraid of?"

She lifted her chin. "I'm not afraid of anything. Good night, Mr. Bradshaw. Have a good weekend." She turned and strode away, her heels clicking against the concrete as she made her way to her Honda.

He followed. "Don't think you're going to get away from me, Vicki." He placed his palm on her car door so she couldn't open it. "I'm ruthless when I want something. And I want you."

Apprehension and excitement skittered across her features before her face grew blank. "We can't always have what we want."

The bitterness in her voice shocked him. There was a story there. One he wanted to get to the bottom of. Then she shouldered his arm out of the way, opened the door, and climbed in. Slamming the door, she started the engine and pushed the old car to its limits as she tore out of the parking lot as if the hounds of hell were nipping at her bumper.

He grinned and sauntered over to his black 'vette. Once inside, he eased down the zipper on his slacks, allowing his cock some breathing room as he pulled out of the parking lot.

Vicki did that to him. Made him hot and hard. She'd done it from the first time he'd seen her on the seventeenth floor, blonde hair tight against her head, only a little makeup, and the loose, drab suit, all intended to disguise her sexuality. He wasn't fazed by it. He had looked beneath the surface right away, and he had known he wanted her. He'd fantasized about all the ways he'd have her. On the desk, the floor, tied up on his bed, against the wall … the list grew bigger and bigger. Then to find out she wore garters … his instincts were correct. Beneath the drab exterior lay a sensual woman.

Getting her alone had shot his control straight to hell. He hadn't planned on an elevator for their encounter. One thing he was sure of, he wasn't sorry he'd fucked her. He could still smell the musky scent of her arousal, the feel of her satin skin against his fingers, and the way her pussy had tightened around his cock.

He was sorry he'd had to wear a condom. Just the thought of feeling her squeezing his bare cock was almost more than he could handle, causing drops of pre-cum to drip on his pants.

But it was more than sex. He liked her spirit. He'd noticed how she interacted with the staff, helped them and never belittled them like some people did. She always had a kind word or smile.

The car wandered into the opposite lane on the winding road to his secluded home outside Seattle, forcing him to concentrate on his driving and not on thoughts of Vicki's lush body. When he reached the top of his hill, he pressed the button and the gate opened. Security lights shone bright as he pulled in front of the sprawling white house sitting in its majestic splendor at the end of the circular driveway.

He zipped up and stepped out of his car, pausing to enjoy the night air. The scents of jasmine and pine filled the evening. The landscaping had been done to his specifications. Stone paths, pine trees planted every twelve feet apart, and jasmine in the backyard around the pool area. Even in the dark, he knew every path to the garden, the pool, and the tennis courts.

When he'd bought the place more than ten years ago, the

house had just been built. He was tired of living in apartments with bothersome neighbors. He wanted a place he could come home to and feel free to do what he wanted, without worrying about who was watching or listening.

He stepped into the entry hall, flipped on the lights, and turned off the security system. The overhead chandelier lit up the room. Right in front of him was the hardwood staircase; off to the left was the chef's kitchen with a big island and plenty of room to cook. The dining room was big enough for dinner parties; to the right lay the living room with its perfect oak chairs and plush sofas for entertaining, while the family room had sofas and big comfy chairs to watch the 65-inch flat-screen TV. Beyond lay his office, which had every modern piece of technology available.

He still marveled at how far he'd come after starting off as a wet-behind-the-ears kid playing with computers. His carefree and careless life had ended when he was approached about a job with a company called Intelligence.

Within seven years, he'd become the CEO. Intent on his career, he'd invested most of his money. After selling his interest in Intelligence at a huge profit, he'd worked as a consultant, only taking the jobs he was interested in. When TechTronics approached him with an offer of a one-year contract for an obscene amount of money, he'd taken it because he wanted to spend more time at his home and he liked the challenge of creating something beyond company expectations.

His thoughts returned to Vicki. She was the marketing manager at TechTronics and their paths crossed on a regular basis. She was another challenge, one he was looking forward to experiencing. Rubbing his hands together, he bounded up the stairs to his bedroom, his cock still heavy with need.

He couldn't wait until he had her alone again. This time he'd prefer someplace more private than the elevator. His bedroom would be a good choice. For a moment, he could imagine her spread-eagled on his bed, her nipples taut with clamps on them, her pussy glistening. He'd approach her at a snail's pace, making her squirm against the black Egyptian cotton sheets in anticipation.

Would she accept his kink? Her boldness in the elevator gave him hope, but he couldn't rush this. Shaking his head, he moved across the room. As he unfastened his pants, his palm brushed against the pocket. Reaching inside, he removed Vicki's hair clip and held it up to the light. The design was intricate and unusual, old-looking. Did she find it in an antique store, or had it been a present? She'd asked for it back, yet he'd distracted her. He hadn't meant to keep it, but now he was glad he had.

Setting the clip on his dresser, he began to push down his pants when he realized there was something in his other pocket. Pulling out the scrap of lace, he smiled and tossed it onto his dresser. Her panties were just like Vicki, sexy and fragile.

He finished taking off his clothes, then sauntered back downstairs. He enjoyed being able to wander around his house naked. Privacy was a privilege he enjoyed. He headed for the kitchen and then grabbed a beer from the fridge. Cold air from the subzero refrigerator made him shiver. Popping the cap off the bottle, he took a long swig. His body still hummed from being with her. He wanted more. And there wasn't a whole lot in life he couldn't get. He had money and looks, and he used them to get what he wanted. But with Vicki, he wanted her to see him as a man, not just as his bad-boy persona.

She had aroused his curiosity. She tried to avoid attention. Perhaps that is what attracted his attention. Her outward appearance was not adorned so as to attract a man's attention, but it had drawn his notice immediately. Her muted clothes and lack of makeup extended to her interactions. In meetings, she was quiet and only answered questions when they were directed at her.

For some reason, Vicki was content not to be noticed. She was bright and she was beautiful, but she didn't want anyone to realize it. Why? The mystery of her drew him as much as her quiet beauty.

The memory of holding her in his arms warmed him. Still naked, he ambled from the kitchen into his office. The soft leather caressed his skin as he sank down onto the executive chair. He turned on his computer and started searching for the information he needed about Vicki. Amazing what you could find on the Internet these days.

Vicki had no idea who she was up against. Joe hadn't gotten his bad-boy reputation playing by the rules. He was a man who knew what he wanted, and he would use means fair and foul to get it.

He wanted her in his house, in every room, and in every position. But it was more than sex. He wanted to know what was going on in her mind as well. He would delve into her secrets using the oldest weapon in the book. Romance was the way to a woman's heart.

WHAT THE HELL had she done? She'd had mind-blowing, wild sex with Joe Bradshaw, that's what. Shame and embarrassment swept their way from her toes to her face. She had promised herself no more work entanglements. Joe was a complication she couldn't afford. Yet she couldn't deny a part of her reveled in the memories of Joe Bradsahw's hands on her body, cock in her pussy—

The sign for Poway Avenue in her headlights jerked her back to the present, and she took the exit, easing her sedan off Main. The sign for Ed's appeared. The dampness between her thighs reminded her of her missing piece of clothing, and the hole-in-the-wall restaurant shrank in the rearview mirror. She needed to get home, back to her safe little world. Slapping a hand against the steering wheel, she muttered, "What was I thinking?" She waited until the light turned green. "That was the problem. I wasn't thinking, I let the wild woman inside rule."

Stupid, stupid, stupid. Hadn't she learned her lesson with Derek?

Thank goodness traffic was light. It only took her thirty minutes to reach her apartment building. She used her security card to open the gate to the garage and pulled her car into its parking space. As she got out of the vehicle, she ran her hands over the wool gabardine of her skirt, smoothing the garment.

After climbing the short flight of stairs, she inserted her card and waited for the light to flash. One of the reasons she'd chosen this apartment building was because you couldn't get in without security card access. The on-duty guard made guests wait in the lobby until the tenant came down to collect them. "Good evening, George," she called in an artificially cheery voice as she walked past the older, balding man.

"Evening, Miss Collins," he replied.

Victoria stopped at her mailbox and extracted her mail, then walked to the elevator bank. Her breath caught in her throat as images of her and Joe flashed before her eyes. Shit, this wasn't good. He wasn't going back in the box of "quickie." One-elevator stand instead of a one-night stand? Her lips twitched inappropriately. This was serious; she shouldn't be laughing at what she'd just done to her career.

The light above the elevator door announced its arrival on the first floor. Two people came out. reminding her how lucky she'd been not to get caught. Had the office guard guessed? At least no one they worked with had been in the lobby when they arrived. She was positive her face had been stamped with the look of a satisfied woman.

The elevator doors started to close.

Suck it up. Unless you want to climb ten flights of stairs, you have no choice but to get in the elevator. She thrust her arm between the closing doors, trigging them to re-open. Biting her lower lip, she forced her shaky legs to budge. Once inside she punched the button for her floor, trying to ignore her racing heart. *Get a grip.*

Her apartment elevator had never gotten stuck before. Still, she let out a breath of relief when the door opened on the tenth floor. The last thing she needed was to replay of tonight.

Reaching her door at the end of the hall, she'd never been so glad to be home. Inserting the key into the first deadbolt, then into the second one, and at last unlocking the doorknob restored her peace of mind. The moment she stepped into her apartment, she flipped on the light. A dejected meow greeted her. "Oh, Sly. I'm so sorry." The gray tomcat entwined his sleek body around her feet. "I didn't think I'd be so late." She pushed the door shut with her foot before leaning down and rubbing her cat behind the ears in apology. Sly hated being left in the dark, and she didn't like coming home to an unlit apartment, either. She really needed to get a timer for the lamp so she wouldn't have to worry anymore.

Straightening, she turned and threw the two deadbolts, locked the door, and secured the chains. Then she dropped her purse and keys onto the entry table and glanced into her small living room. She paused. Was it always as unappealing as it seemed tonight? She stared at her furniture. Maybe it was the way the beige carpet and beige sofa almost blended together, or how uniform the pictures were on one wall. Or how there wasn't anything reflecting her personality in the room. No family pictures, no knickknacks; everything was functional.

A sigh escaped her. Had she suppressed so much since Derek? Yes, it looked like she had. She sighed again. After Derek's destructiveness, she hadn't replaced any of her stuff. Fear of his finding her and going on a rampage held her back. She stared out the window, seeking a glimpse of the calming waters of the Puget

Sound. Lights glistening off the smooth water calmed her nerves. Derek was still out there somewhere, but she hoped never to see him again. Unfortunately, her ex-fiancé wasn't getting the message. He kept calling her at home and leaving messages. She glanced at her answering machine with dread in her belly.

Yep, the little red light was flashing. Striding over, she hit the playback button. Listening to the messages was her way of knowing his state of mind. And it was the only evidence she had right now to turn over to the police. When the calls had first started, she had talked to the police, but there wasn't much they could do. She'd changed her phone number four times, and still Derek found it. Even after talking with a lawyer again, there was no evidence, so she'd bought an old-fashioned answering machine to record him on tape.

Derek's whining voice began speaking. "Pick up the phone, Victoria. I want to talk to you. Why won't you answer me? I miss you. Call me." *Beep*, then the next one started. "Come on, Victoria, you know you love me." *Beep*. "What the fuck is the matter?" he roared, making her whole body cringe in fear. "Why aren't you calling me back?" *Beep*. Then the last one. "I think your marketing report has gone missing. I'll get you fired from this job, too, if you don't call me back."

Victoria's stomach clenched, then she sighed with relief at the knowledge the marketing report was safely in the VP's office. But how had Derek known about it? Fear coiled in her belly.

She took a deep breath to calm herself. She was safe right now. That's what counted. She didn't need to dream up more things to fear.

At least tonight there were only four calls. Maybe he was beginning to get the message. In the beginning, she would come home to ten or twelve messages every night. She knew if she didn't respond to Derek, he'd get tired and give up. She didn't want any more trouble. Derek had a way of making everything look like it was her fault. Losing her job had been enough. And based on Derek's message, she needed to be more careful in the future. She'd check in with her lawyer again to see if there was anything at all he could do.

She flipped through her mail and noticed the familiar handwriting leaping out. Closing her eyes, she sighed again before she pulled the tape out of her answering machine and put it with the letter into the almost overflowing drawer of tapes and letters. Her apartment complex was safe and secure. Derek hadn't been in physical contact with her and at this point the courts wouldn't issue an order of protection. She and Derek were through. Pushing aside thoughts of her disastrous engagement, she moved into the kitchen and glanced at the clock on the microwave.

Nine o'clock. She'd been stuck in the elevator for more than an hour. She hadn't noticed, not with Joe distracting her. Her nipples hardened. She didn't want memories of Joe's touch, the feel of his skin against hers, in possession of her mind right now. All she wanted was to take a shower, put on her favorite nightshirt, climb into bed, and forget everything. Derek, Joe, her job—just for a night of peace.

After opening the cabinet, she pulled out some dry cat food and a bag of cat crunchies. In a gesture of apology, she gave Sly more treats than customary and filled his bowl with fresh water. Since her cat was satisfied, she could ... what?

Joe had pleasured her sexually, so why did she feel so empty, so alone? *Oh, snap out of it, Victoria. You wanted the man; you got him. It's over; you don't need to do a post mortem.* Straightening her shoulders, she made her way down the small hallway to her bedroom.

After clicking on the lamp by her bed, she kicked off her shoes and removed her jacket. A lock of hair fell into her eyes, reminding her of the absence of her clip. Her clip! Joe still had it.

She'd asked him for it then forgotten about it. Another thing to be ashamed of, losing her grandmother's clip. Well, she'd get it back from him on Monday. No way was she going to let embarrassment about what they did together in the elevator get the better of her. The clip was a precious gift.

Her stomach tumbled. Her clip and her torn panties—he had them both. Wrapping her arms around herself, she tried not to feel like a piece of her was missing. Between her missing hair adornment and her panties, a part of her soul was missing. Joe had carved a piece of it and now held it in his possession. Male possession …

With a toss of her head, she shook off her misgivings about what she'd done. Joe's form of possession was totally different from Derek's. Joe made her feel like a treasure to possess, not an object to be abused. And she was a big girl. She had the right to enjoy her body with a man she desired. Joe's hungry gaze, the way he savored every inch of her with his tongue and hands, was nothing like the slaps and hurting grips of Derek.

Yes, Joe was a powerful man who went after what he wanted, but he waited for her consent. Was she nuts to trust him? No. She wouldn't let Derek take the natural trust between two consenting adults away from her. He'd already taken more than enough. Her job, her sense of safety, even her style.

She crossed to the old-fashioned dresser and pulled out a soft, well-worn purple nightshirt and a pair of purple satin panties. Inside the bathroom, she locked the door, then undressed, dropping the dirty clothes into the hamper before stepping into the shower.

The hot water felt good against her skin. She closed her eyes and let the water pour over her body, washing away Joe's scent. Part of her was saddened to lose his smell; the other part reminded her it was all for the best. If only it was so easy to wash away the memories. She still remembered the way his hands felt on her breasts, tweaking her nipples, making them pulse with need. And his lips roaming over her skin, nipping and licking, and his cock … She snapped her eyes open. Her fingers were at her nipples, plucking them into hardness.

Enough! She wasn't going to start fantasizing about him. Not again. She didn't need a man in her life, let alone Joe Bradshaw, a bad-boy colleague. She finished her shower, then enveloped herself in a fluffy white towel. Picking up the hand towel on the counter, she used a corner of the cloth to wipe off the mirror and stared at her reflection.

Her blonde hair was a mess. Tomorrow she'd wash her hair; it was too late tonight. She didn't want to go to bed with wet hair, and she didn't have the energy to blow dry and style it tonight. Her pupils were enlarged, her cheeks flushed, and her lips swollen. She looked like a woman who'd just left her lover's bed. Great. The guard had probably noticed. But, thank God, no one else had seen her mussed state.

Because she had indeed just left her lover's arms, if one-time wild sex in the elevator made them lovers. She tilted her head. Yes, they were lovers. Ah, hell, this isn't what she wanted to be thinking, not right now.

A tingling started at her toes and moved its way through her body. She recognized it as anticipation—anticipation of the next time she and Joe would be together. No! There wasn't going to be a next time. There couldn't be. While Joe was used to getting his own way on the business side of things, she'd had enough of domineering men in her life.

Lovers.

Stop it. She pushed all thoughts of Joe and sex out of her mind, brushed her teeth, and dried off. By the time she'd put on her panties and nightshirt, she was back under control and feeling less vulnerable.

The beige carpet tickled her bare feet as she strode into her bedroom. She folded back the patchwork quilt to reveal the red satin sheets. The cool satin made her skin prickle with a chill, but once the comforter trapped her body heat, the fabric warmed to a caress.

Once she was warm she liked the occasional shock of rolling over into a cold section of the sheets. Cold against warm skin brought an instant of … not pain—but unpleasantness, and an instant later, pleasure.

She turned off the light. The night light in the bathroom gave off just enough of a glow to chase away the shadows. Until Derek, she had never needed a night light, even as a child.

She rolled onto her back and stared up at the ceiling. Thank goodness tomorrow was Saturday and she wouldn't have to face work or Joe. A day to catch up on housework and laundry. She squirmed against the slick fabric. She had two days to figure out how to handle him. Not a lot of time, but it was better than nothing.

Her big gray cat, Sly, jumped on the bed with a thump and padded over, nudging her hand. "Happy?" She scratched him behind the ears. He curled up against her side and began purring. Victoria smiled and closed her eyes. Tomorrow she'd see things more clearly, without the afterglow of great sex clouding her judgment.

VICTORIA TOSSED ASIDE the tangled sheets and glanced at the clock. Six. No wonder it was still dark. With a sigh, she sat up. It was all Joe Bradshaw's fault. He'd invaded her mind, her body, and now her dreams. She ached all over, not only from the elevator sex, but from the unfulfilled dreams and a body throbbing with need.

What had made her think having sex with Joe would cure her of him? Instead, it had only made her want him more, and she didn't like it. She rose and meandered barefoot down the carpeted hallway to the kitchen.

She was going to need extra caffeine today. With precision she measured out the grounds and poured the water into the coffeemaker. While she waited for the coffee to percolate, her mind processed the events of the previous evening once again.

While she'd like to tell herself Joe had seduced her, she couldn't. She'd been a willing participant. Hell, she'd been eager for his touch, his kisses, his cock. She wanted him as much as he wanted her, and that's all there was to it.

Maybe going so long without sex hadn't been a good idea. Staying celibate seemed the safest course after Derek, but ... Another sigh slipped past her lips. She'd fallen into her relationship with him, one of comfort, at least in the beginning. Then Derek began to change, becoming more possessive, more destructive. She'd tolerated things. Was she doing that with Joe? Could she trust her own judgment? Especially when she was so powerfully attracted to him?

The percolator gave its last gasp, signaling the coffee was ready. The rich aromas and steam counteracted the ice in her veins at the thought of Joe changing like Derek had. No, they were different. Or was she fooling herself?

After pouring a cup, she collected the throw blanket from the sofa and stepped out onto the small balcony.

Careful not to spill and stain the cream-colored throw, she set her coffee cup on the tiny table. Then she lowered herself onto the love seat and curled her legs beneath her, cuddling into the throw around her shoulders. The coffee was rich with chocolate and coconut. German chocolate—her favorite flavor. There was only one coffee shop downtown that carried the brew, and she picked up a pound at the first of every month.

She watched as the black sky lightened to gray, then yellow, and then light blue, which reminded her of Joe's eyes. Digging her fingers into the angora, she pulled it around the gap at her neck, nudging out the early morning chill.

What was she going to do about Joe? There wasn't much she could do. A one-time thing, that's what it was. Over and done with. And there was no going back to before it happened. The deed was done. She couldn't undo what she'd done. Pressure built against the backside of her ribs.

No, this wasn't the same situation as with Derek. It wasn't like she and Joe had been involved and then broke up. Losing her job had been because of what Derek had done. Joe wasn't like that, she was sure. Derek was a jerk.

She'd have to play it way cool at work and outside of work as well. Office affairs were never secret for long. Even though Joe had indicated he wanted more, it wasn't a good idea.

Was she smiling? She giggled and buried her nose in the soft fabric of her throw. If their compatibility was determined by sex, there was definitely a future there. Last night had been wildfire. Of course Joe wanted more. She did too—but that wasn't the point. Joe—and any man or woman, for that matter—would want more of what they'd enjoyed last night.

She wiped the smirk off her face. Playing with fire was the last thing she should be doing if she didn't want to lose her job and have to find another one.

No, the problem with her and Joe wasn't sex, it was their working for the same company. Unlike Derek, Joe wasn't her boss, but it might be seen as unprofessional for them to see each other. And Derek? She was tired of him. Tired of his harassment. But what could she do when she had no legal options? They'd been good together once. In the beginning of their relationship, Derek had helped her through the terrible period following her grandmother's death. He was a good-looking man and he'd been kind and caring, taking care of her every need. Then he changed. It was slow at first, a comment here and there. Hating her clothing, the way her hair looked, saying she wore too much makeup or too little. When she began to notice the changes in him, she was in too deep. Until the last night, when he had slapped her. She had already begun to think about leaving him, but when he hit her, that sealed the deal. She walked out and a weight lifted from her shoulders. But Derek wanted her back, and that was never going to happen. But she wouldn't let Joe get in the middle of her mess.

Victoria took a deep breath and let it out. She needed to get her mind off both men. Since it was Saturday, she might as well clean her apartment and do laundry. Yep, that was the ticket. A little physical work would make her feel better. She drained the last of her coffee and surged to her feet.

BY TEN, HER apartment was spotless. She'd finished folding the last of her laundry. While the sense of satisfaction made her smile, now what was she going to do for the rest of the day? Joe's image rose in her mind. She closed her eyes and willed the vision away. Even while she was doing housework, Joe was never very far from her mind.

It annoyed her she couldn't stop her body from reacting to her thoughts.

The doorbell rang, and for a second her pulse kicked up a notch. *Don't be silly.* He couldn't get by the security guard; perhaps it was a neighbor. Crossing the room, she peeked through the peephole.

"Joe!" Her heart started pounding. Her fingers trembled as she undid the multiple chains and locks. This was a bad idea, but knowing that didn't stop her.

When at last she pulled open the door, he greeted her with a wide smile. "Good morning."

"How … " She broke off when she saw Phil, the day guard, out of the corner of her eyes. "Good morning, Phil."

"Morning, Ms. Collins. Mr. Bradshaw wanted to surprise you, so I brought him up. It's okay, isn't it?"

Victoria opened her mouth to remind Phil about the rules, but Joe spoke before she could.

"Sweetheart, I told Phil you'd just forgotten to put my name on the guest list since we just started dating." He ran his fingers down her arm, leaving goose bumps from his soft touch.

She fought not to moan at the sensation of his skin against hers. She glanced over at Phil, who shifted from one foot to the other. "It's okay, Phil. Thank you for escorting Joe up here and making sure everything was all right." Phil nodded, then walked away. The minute the elevator doors closed, Victoria looked back at Joe. "What are you doing here?"

"That's my Vicki, straight to the point." His grin widened. His black shirt and black jeans molded to his body, giving him the ultimate bad-boy look. "Invite me in."

"No." She'd only opened the door to figure out how he had gotten past security. Wasn't it bad enough he'd invaded her mind and her dreams? Now he wanted to invade her apartment. No way.

Joe shrugged. "I can discuss last night out here in the hall." He glanced to his left as a door opened.

Victoria caught sight of one of the two young children who lived next door peering out. "Joe," she started. She couldn't let him rehash last night.

"How are you feeling?" He trailed his fingers over her cheek. "Was I too rough last night?"

Once again, her skin tingled where he touched her, but his words made her tremble. This wasn't a conversation she wanted anyone to overhear, let alone a kid. The boys' mother stepped into the hallway, holding her younger child by the hand. Victoria's heart clenched.

"Good morning," Joe said when her neighbor walked past Vicki's door.

"Good morning," the woman replied with an excessively friendly smile.

Victoria rolled her eyes and stepped back so Joe could enter her apartment. Once he crossed the threshold, she pushed the door shut and leaned against it. Only then did she allow her gaze to cover him from head to toe.

His blue eyes danced with mischief. The black polo-style shirt accentuated his broad shoulders, and the black jeans molded to his thighs, reminding her of just how strong his legs were. "Like what you see?" The amusement in his voice caused her gaze to snap up to his face. She was acting like a teenager ogling the quarterback.

"Yes, I do." Why couldn't she lie? No, she had to blurt out the truth. "What do you want, Joe?"

"Two things." He reached into his pocket. "First, to give you this." He held out his hand.

"My clip." Her heart turned over. She'd forgotten all about it this morning. Her hand rose and she took it from his palm, not quite able to ignore the heat from his skin. "Thank you." She closed her fingers around the clip and then pressed it against her chest.

"It's very special to you, isn't it?" The mischief in his eyes was replaced with tenderness.

"Yes." She cleared her tight throat. "My grandfather was a silversmith, and he made the clip for my grandmother as a wedding gift. My grandmother gave it to me the day before she died." The memory of her grandmother's death reminded Victoria of her loneliness. Her parents lived out of state and she wasn't close to any of her step-brothers or step-sisters. She fought back the sudden tears.

"I'm sorry." The words were soft as he brushed his thumb across her cheek, catching the lone tear she couldn't stop from falling.

Her breath caught. The compassion and care etched on Joe's face made it hard to get air into her lungs. Derek had never shown any such consideration for her feelings. She allowed herself the luxury of his soft touch for one more moment. Then she tilted her head, moving away from his hand. "She's been gone almost two years, but sometimes it still seems like yesterday."

That's when her life started going downhill. Meeting Derek, his possessiveness, getting fired. And the spiral had continued until she had come to work at TechTronics. The thought of work made her spine stiffen. She couldn't afford to forget she and Joe worked for the same company. She'd learned from her mistakes.

Swallowing, she scooted around him. "I'll just go put this away."

Joe watched Vicki scurry out of the room and longed to follow her. When a lone tear had trailed down her cheek, his gut had tightened. She needed tenderness and compassion, and he wanted to give her everything. Not something he usually wanted to do for a sexual partner, but Vicki was different. There was an air of fragility to her, but also a spine of steel. He looked forward to sparring with her in and out of bed.

He strode into the living room area, glanced at the beige sofa, and smiled. Clothes sat in several piles. Apparently he'd caught her doing laundry. Unable to resist, he moved closer.

Bright scraps of satin were folded and stacked with precision. He wasn't wrong about Vicki being a sensuous woman. The lingerie just added to his confidence. Without conscious thought, he picked up a satin black teddy. He held it out in front of him. Blood rushed from his brain straight south, making him hard.

"Joe!" Her tone was exasperated.

He glanced away from the scrap of silk to see her standing with hands on hips. "Model this for me." He dangled the delicate garment on his finger.

Color swept into her cheeks, and he fought against grinning. She stomped across the room and reached for the teddy. He stepped back. "Give it to me." She blew out a puff of breath in exasperation.

"Only if you wear it for me. Here and now." He wanted to see her in it. His body demanded it, erotic images filling his mind. He knew with exact detail what he would do to her when he stripped the silk from her lush body.

Her jaw clenched. "I think you're under some impression you can order me around, Mr. Bradshaw."

He winced when she called him "mister." But he was determined not to let Victoria hide behind her prim mask. He loved her sexual side. He wanted to make her feel special, wanted, loved. "I want you, Vicki. Is it a bad thing?" She reared back, and he went on the attack. "Because I do want you," he continued. "I've wanted you for months."

This time, she shook her head and lowered her chin to her chest.

He tossed the teddy onto the sofa, took a step forward, and placed his finger beneath her chin. Lifting her head, he noticed the confusion and doubts in her eyes. His gut clenched. He'd thought she'd be on board with him, but apparently something was off. Had he misjudged her? "You're surprised I want you?"

She tried to step away, but he tightened his hold and slipped his free arm around her waist. He didn't pull her close, yet she inhaled sharply at the contact. Silence filled the room while he waited. If need be, he'd wait all day for her answer. "You're not going to let this go, are you?" she asked, her tone soft and resigned.

"No."

"Last night was good."

"More than good. Extraordinary is a better word." It had been extraordinary and unique for him, and he knew he hadn't been alone in feeling that way.

"Can't happen again."

Her words floored him. Did she think he was just looking for a quickie? Yes, she did. He could see it in the way her gaze kept darting away from his and in the stiffness of her body. His gut clenched. Well, he would clear up this little misunderstanding right now.

"You believe I'm here only because I want sex?" He asked the question even though he already knew the answer. He wanted to hear it from her lips.

"Why else would you be here?"

Joe stepped back, forcing himself to release her. He hadn't expected this, and it made him damn uncomfortable that she had such a low opinion of him. Running a hand over his face, he rocked back on his heels and stared at her. "You don't believe I'm here because I'd like to get to know you better?"

"No, I don't." She didn't even hesitate.

"Why?" He was determined to get to the bottom of this. Why did she feel sex was all he had to offer?

Vicki crossed her arms over her chest. "Why would you want anything else?"

"Maybe because I see what's beneath your prickly surface."

She laughed and her eyes narrowed. "Typical male response."

He stared at her. "Are you making me pay for some other man's crime?" Asking her questions wasn't getting him answers, but this one did.

A flash of surprise crossed her features before she could mask it. Bull's-eye. Some man had hurt her. "I think it's time for you to go."

He wasn't about to budge. Not until they had this worked out. "Tell me about him."

Vicki huffed an exasperated sigh. "You just don't get it, do you?" She leaned over the sofa, picked up the teddy, folded it, and placed it on top of the pile before lifting the stack into her arms. "I don't want you here when I get back."

Her butt swayed as she marched away. He wasn't going anywhere except maybe to follow her. He wanted to get to the bottom of why she was trying to push him away. His brain was telling him to leave, but his heart wanted more, to show her how special she was.

Chapter Three

Victoria took more time putting her clothes away than usual, trying to ignore the tremor of excitement flowing through her veins. Joe would be gone by the time she meandered back into the living room. She'd made it clear she didn't want him here. *But I do want him.* Victoria sighed. She couldn't deny her body craved his, but it didn't mean she was going to jump into bed with him. Out of the question. They worked together, plus the whole Derek issue. She wouldn't drag him into her mess.

She pushed the dresser drawer closed, turned, and let out a squeal when she noticed Joe lounging against the doorjamb. "I thought I told you to leave."

"You did."

"Then why are you still here?" Her heartbeat increased. Damn, he was sex on a stick. Her heart fluttered; having him in the doorway of her bedroom caused her pussy to weep.

"I'm not leaving until we hash this out."

"Hash what out?" His scent carried across the room, teasing her. Citrus and masculinity. The smell should have been overpowering, but not on him. Instead it fueled the deep desire streaming through her body. Damn, she so didn't need this. Why was she allowing her emotions to control her? Maybe because she'd been attracted to Joe since he had come to work at TechTronics, or maybe because he called to the side of herself she had buried when she left Derek.

"You're determined not to let me into your life?" His voice was soft as he took a step into the room.

Even with several feet between them, she could feel his magnetism. She wanted nothing more than for him to pull her into his arms, to have his lips on hers, his tongue thrusting into her mouth. "You're too dangerous." The words slipped out before she was even aware of voicing them aloud. Oh, hell's bells, why did she say that?

His eyes widened, and another of those sexy, devilish grins spread across his face. "I'm not dangerous. I'm a teddy bear."

Victoria gave a snort of laughter. He took another step toward her, and now her bedroom felt too small. He was invading her territory. Her heart pounded. She should shoo him out, but he looked good in her bedroom. Another danger sign. "Grizzly bear is more like it," she muttered.

"A man," he said, taking two more steps. "A man who wants to get to know you better."

"If we get to know each other any better, we'll be arrested." Her gaze locked with his as the corner of his mouth twitched. He stood less than a foot away.

Then the corners of his mouth turned down, and his brows drew together as he studied her. "I got things a little backward last night."

"Backward?" An odd word to use. She tilted her head to one side and stared.

"Yep, backward." He caressed her cheek. "Making love to you in the elevator was impulsive."

She opened her mouth to speak.

"But," he continued before she could get a word out, "I don't regret one second of it."

Truth be told, neither did she. She'd never felt so much passion, such fulfillment, such pleasure. She might want to deny it, but knew she couldn't. So much for resisting this sexy man. "Neither do I." She forced the words past the lump in her throat.

"I knew it." He slipped his hand behind her neck.

Shivers coursed through her body at the contact. She leaned toward him. "Joe?"

With a groan, he tugged her into his embrace, his lips finding hers. Her lips parted without hesitation. God, it felt so good to be in his arms once again. This was where she belonged. She shivered as the thought filtered through her brain.

JOE FOUGHT AGAINST the need to devour her. To rip their clothes off, throw her on the bed, and bury himself so deep inside her body neither of them would be able to figure out where one ended and the other began. He smoothed his palms over her well-worn t-shirt. His need for her overwhelmed him, but he'd promised himself in the wee hours of the morning that he'd do this right. He wouldn't overpower her with passion, but here he was kissing her. With reluctance, he broke the kiss and forced himself to step away. Her moan of protest made him gather her back into his arms.

Again their lips came together. Tongues tangled and hands wandered over bodies. She traced his shoulder muscles before sinking deep in his hair while he slid his hand down her back, pulling her body against his.

They parted, but he trailed his lips down her neck, nipping and licking her skin. She tasted so good, fresh like summer rain. Her head fell back as he continued to nuzzle her neck. The pressure against his fly reminded him how far gone he was.

His wants didn't matter. This was about Vicki. About making her feel safe with him, letting her know it was more than just sex. Lifting his head, he waited until she opened her eyes before he spoke. "I'm going to do this right."

"Felt pretty damn right to me." Her voice was soft and dreamy.

"Damn it, woman. You aren't making this easy." He took two steps away, hands clenched at his sides. He had to get some distance before it was too late.

"Who says I want easy?" She followed, cupping his cock.

"Vicki." He ground out her name between clenched teeth. This woman excited him just standing there, let alone touching him. Fighting against his baser needs wasn't simple, but instead of giving in, he grasped her wrist and pulled her tantalizing fingers away. If this was just about sex, he'd have let her continue. The thought sobered him. He *was* going to do this right, damn it. He wanted to show her there was more to him than sex. He wanted a relationship. "Let's go to lunch." He needed to get out of her apartment, and soon. At least in the open he'd be less tempted to strip her naked. He hoped.

She blinked several times as she tried to catch up with his change of subject. "Okay, just let me … " She glanced down and let out a squeal. "Oh, my God, I'm a mess."

"You're beautiful." Disbelief blazed in her green eyes. Grasping her by the shoulders, holding her in place, he said, "Very beautiful."

"How can I be? I'm in old sweats and a baggy t-shirt."

"Because you are." His words were husky with need. His chest swelled as he took a deep breath, then he cradled her hands in his. "You are sexy and beautiful no matter what you're wearing. It isn't the clothes, Vicki, it's you."

"Oh, Joe." She swayed toward him, desire and need in her

gaze.

"Not now, sweetheart." He kept her at arm's length. Self-preservation was at the top of the list. "I have very little control where you're concerned. I'll wait in the living room since you want to change." He dropped a kiss on her nose before releasing her and striding out.

"WHERE ARE WE going?" she asked, as he drove his Mercedes across town. Her body still hummed with joy at his presence. She knew she should resist him, but she couldn't. She'd take it a day at a time and worry about the consequences later because she wanted to see if there was something more than sex with Joe.

"Just a little place I know."

"And the name of it is?"

"Marco's." He pulled the car into an almost empty lot.

The area wasn't run down, but it wasn't affluent, either. Why was she surprised? Maybe because she kept seeing Joe surrounded by only the best. She reached for the door handle.

"Sit still." He said, before hopping out of the car and crossing to her side. She waited for him to open her door, then took his offered hand and allowed him to help her from the vehicle.

Drawing her arm through his, he led her around the littered asphalt to a door. There was a simple sign hanging above it that read 'Marco's.'

The dim interior made her blink several times before her eyes adjusted. When they did, she noticed an elevator. Surprised, she looked up at Joe with her stomach clenched. He smiled while he punched the up button.

"Don't worry," he said. "No elevator ravishment."

Her cheeks grew hot, and his lips tilted in amusement. The elevator arrived with a moan and groan. They stepped inside when the doors opened.

"At least not today," he added; his eyes gleamed.

The car began to rise, and after a moment the elevator halted with a shudder and the doors opened. Victoria felt her mouth form an "O." The restaurant wasn't what she had expected.

Light and open space greeted them. Tables with gleaming white cloths and small candles as centerpieces were spread over the polished wood floors, while the floor-to-ceiling windows made use of the natural light, making the entire place feel spacious and open.

"Joe!" a male voice bellowed. "It's great to see you." A large man bore down on them. Smiling, he took Joe's hand and pumped it several times.

"Hey, Marco."

"And who is this lovely woman?" His brown eyes focused on her.

"Vicki, meet Marco, an old friend and owner of this establishment." There was pride in Joe's voice.

"It's nice to meet you, Vicki." Marco took her hand and kissed the back of it before returning his attention to Joe. "You were always lucky with women."

"Yeah."

Victoria was amazed to see a bit of red creep into Joe's face. Deciding to take the unwanted attention off Joe, she commented, "This is a beautiful place, Marco."

"Thanks to Joe. Come on, let me get you seated before the lunch crowd gets here." Marco led them across the room to a table next to one of the large windows. "I'll be right back with a bottle of wine," Marco said, laying the menus on the table.

Victoria looked out over Seattle at the water of Puget Sound in the distance. "The view is great," she said, turning back to face Joe.

"Without a doubt."

She bit her lip. Her other question slipped from her mind. Joe was looking at her, not out the window. Heat filled her veins at being the center of his attention. How did one deal with a man like him? *With caution.* She reached for one of the menus.

Joe captured her hand. Her gaze met his. Blue as the sky and as deep as the sea, his eyes were pools she could drown in. "Vicki." He lifted her fingers to his lips, kissing each tip, creating a delicious heat throughout her body. "We're going to have lunch and talk, and what happens after is up to you."

"No pressure?"

"None whatsoever. If you want me to take you home, I'll respect your wishes."

Her eyes widened. "What's changed?"

"Nothing." He kept her hand enclosed within his.

"Something has." She swallowed. "You don't take no for an answer."

"Mostly true."

"Okay, not from women, anyway."

His eyebrows rose at the sarcasm in her voice. "I've never met a woman like you."

"You don't need to flatter me." Wasn't this how her relationship started with Derek? There were some parallels, but if she was honest with herself, Joe was nothing like Derek.

He gave a quick, dry laugh. "It's not flattery; it's the truth." His eyes narrowed and he tightened his hand around hers. "You've captured my attention like no other woman has." His tone was low and deep.

"I didn't mean to." A tremor swept through her body at his words.

"That's for sure. In those conservative clothes, always avoiding being alone with me, yet watching me from the corner of your eyes in fascination. It's been impossible for me to concentrate when you're in the room."

She shook her head in disbelief. "You never showed it."

"How could I? At first, I thought it was a game to you." He grimaced.

"I don't play games."

"After last night, I know." His features softened. "I watched you watching me, and it gave me hope. It was only a matter of time before I made a move."

"So last night wasn't planned?" Her heart lightened.

This time his laugh was full-blooded. "You give me a lot of credit for causing the elevator to stop."

This time she couldn't help but smile. "I didn't mean to imply you stopped the elevator."

"Making love to you there wasn't part of my plan, but the opportunity presented itself and I answered the call." A small grin played around his lips. "It was magical."

"Here we go." Marco interrupted before she could question Joe further. "One of my best Merlots." He opened the bottle with a flourish.

VICTORIA COULDN'T REMEMBER having a more satisfying and fun lunch. Marco waited on them with personal flair, even when his restaurant began to fill up. Feeling pampered and happy for the first time in a long time, she began to relax.

"How about a walk around Shilshole Bay?" Joe asked as they pulled out of the parking lot.

"Good idea. After all the delicious food, I need some exercise."

They stopped at a red light, and his gaze swept her from head to toe. "Not as far as I'm concerned."

Heat filled her. Without conscious thought she leaned toward him. Their lips touched for a brief moment before a horn honked. Joe swore and hit the accelerator, as the light had changed to green.

The car was filled with charged silence. Joe drove as if he were one with his car and parked near the Shilshole Bay Marina. Without a word, he exited the vehicle and walked around the front of the car. Opening the door, he offered his hand.

Victoria slipped her hand into his, and a zing of excitement raced up her spine. But all he did was smile and lock the car. They began walking hand in hand. "I don't think I've been here before," she said, realizing she hadn't gotten out to explore Seattle since she moved here three years ago.

"Then you're in for a treat."

The day had turned out to be beautiful. Victoria enjoyed feeling the sun's warmth on her face and how crystal clear the sky was. She was even more amazed they could see the Olympic Mountains; she hadn't realized they were so close. She drank in the beautiful snow-capped mountains.

"How long have you lived in the Seattle area?" she asked as Joe guided her away from a roller-blading couple.

"About three years."

"Where did you live before?" She was curious about him.

"Boston."

"And—"

He pulled her to a stop and pressed his fingers against her lips. "I'm thirty-four, never married, my parents are still alive and living in Boston, and I'm an only child."

Her cheeks grew warm. "I didn't mean to pry," she mumbled against his fingers.

"Shhh." He cupped her chin. "I thought it'd be easier to get the basics out of the way." He dropped a soft kiss on her lips, but to her regret, it was over way too soon.

She decided to reciprocate because the darn man was so charming and she was comfortable around him. "I grew up in a small town in Illinois. My dad still lives there, and my mom lives in Florida." She wasn't about to mention the passel of half-brothers and half-sisters she had. Her parents were not known for their staying power in marriage.

"How long have you been in Seattle?" he asked as they resumed their walk.

"Not long, about three years. I moved here to help take care of my grandmother."

"The grandmother who died?"

"Yes." Vicki swallowed the lump in her throat. "I was able to spend almost two years with her before she passed."

"I'm sorry." His fingers laced with hers and squeezed.

"Thanks. Grandma was pragmatic to the end, saying she was ready and couldn't wait to be with Grandpa again so they could have some nookie."

Joe's rich laugher made her grin. "Interesting woman, your grandmother."

"Yes, she was. She would have liked you; you're nothing like D—" She broke off and looked away. She didn't want to spoil her time with Joe by mentioning Derek. Besides, today would probably be the only date she and Joe had, based on Derek's past actions. Derek had a way of making any man she dated suddenly lose interest in her. With a shake of her head, she dispelled all thoughts of her ex. "So, tell me." She pasted a bright smile on her face. "Why did you come to Seattle?"

Joe raised an eyebrow at the questions, but all she did was keep the smile plastered on her face. After a second or two he answered. "I have a home here, and TechTronics made me an offer I couldn't refuse."

Vicki breathed a sigh of relief as they continued to talk as they strolled. She couldn't remember a more pleasant time in her life. At one point, they'd stopped for a drink. She could have sworn she caught a glimpse of a man who looked like Derek not too far from them. Unease slid through her, and she couldn't help but to keep her gaze on the crowd of people.

"Something wrong?" Joe looked around with a frown.

In a blink, the man was gone. "Nothing, just my imagination." And that's all it was, her imagination. She was sure of it.

As they walked back to the car, they came upon a little girl who had fallen off her bike. Victoria's heart melted as Joe knelt beside the child, talking to her in a soft voice and making sure she was okay before helping her up and back onto her bicycle. The little girl sang Joe's praises when her mother ran up to them.

As she stood there, Victoria realized it would be very easy to fall in love with Joe Bradshaw. Oh, Lord, she couldn't fall in love, not until she had her head on straight and Derek permanently out of her life.

Chapter Four

Sitting at her desk Monday morning, Victoria rubbed her temples. A headache had lodged there and refused to leave. Arousal still throbbed through her body, and it hadn't given her a moment's peace since her encounter with Joe over the weekend. But Joe wasn't the cause of her headache—Derek was. Saturday he'd left more messages on her machine, and on Sunday there were more, warning her that she belonged to him and any man in her life wouldn't last long. None of them ever had before.

She forced thoughts of Derek away. She didn't want to think about him now. Instead, she focused her mind on Joe. True to his word, he hadn't pushed. He had left her at her door with a chaste kiss. He'd called on Sunday, which left her wanting more of his company.

She'd had to replace the batteries in her vibrator twice over the weekend. She was beginning to feel her resolve weakening, and she didn't like it one bit.

Victoria still didn't understand what had happened on Friday night. She hadn't done drugs or been drunk beforehand. She'd been tired and vulnerable, but those feelings didn't explain abandoning her normal principles to have elevator sex with a man she didn't know. Then to go out with him on Saturday …

She rubbed her forehead. Was being without sex all of the last year a bad idea? Maybe if she'd fooled around a little, Joe wouldn't have affected her as much. But deep down inside, she knew it wasn't true. He had an ability to read her, to see the woman she hid beneath the conservative suits and cool attitude. He dug deeper when other men only skimmed the surface. It unnerved her and yet excited her.

She remembered the twinkle in his eyes when he'd teased her, his husky chuckle and the utterly masculine groan when she'd taken his cock in her mouth. *Stop it!* She shifted in her chair, trying to relieve the throbbing between her legs. She opened the next email.

A gasp left her lips. It was a picture of her and Joe at the café where they'd had a drink on Saturday. The words "You're mine" danced before her eyes. Without thinking, she reached for the phone, but her fingers never got past the first few digits. What could the police do? Maybe she should talk with the IT guys. No. She didn't want to involve anyone in the company. She dropped the receiver back into place.

This was her problem. She wouldn't bring anyone else into the mess of her life. She pressed her knuckles against her eyelids, trying to regain her focus, but her insides quaked.

A knock on her door captured her attention as the door opened and her assistant, Lisa, stepped into the room. "Monthly meeting in five minutes."

"Thanks. I forgot all about it." With a couple clicks of her mouse, the email was moved to a special file, and she stood. "Anything I need to worry about?"

"No." Lisa smiled, holding out a folder. "All routine."

"Good." Victoria took the folder and headed up to the eighteenth-floor conference room. She had forgotten about the monthly department meeting, not that there was much for her to report. She'd just turned in the marketing report to the president on Friday.

She strode into the room and stopped in her tracks. Joe stood by the coffee carafe talking with Will from shipping. Damn, the man looked all sexy, his hair tussled as if he'd just woken up.

He glanced up. A wide smile graced his lips, and she lost her breath, feeling the impact of his grin all the way to her toes. Victoria found her composure and marched into the room.

After setting her folder down on the table, she made her way over to the refreshment table. Joe was still standing there.

"Good morning, Victoria."

"Mr. Bradshaw." She reached for a cup.

"Joe, remember." His breath caressed her skin.

Her hand trembled as she filled the cup with coffee. "You're too close," she whispered.

"Not close enough."

She opened her mouth to retort when Jessica Neimier sashayed into the room and straight over to them. "Good morning, Joe." Her dark red nails against Joe's tan forearm caused Victoria to tense.

What the hell was wrong with her? Joe didn't belong to her. They'd had sex, yes. They'd technically gone on a date Saturday, yes. But sex and one date wasn't a relationship.

Just then the president strolled into the room. "Good morning, everyone. Shall we get started?"

Victoria nodded at Joe before taking her seat. To her surprise, Joe sat down next to her. This wasn't unusual, but today his body heat called to her. Fighting the impulse to wrap herself in his arms, she opened her folder, picked up a pen, and began taking notes.

Joe kept an eye on Vicki as the meeting started. While there wasn't a hair out of place, something was off. She was tense. Who was he kidding? She was like a damn statue sitting next to him.

Was she worried he'd do something on the job? Even if he did, it would be away from prying eyes. What he had with Vicki was his business and no one else's. He'd hoped after their time together on Saturday and then his talking to her on Sunday, she'd be more relaxed around him.

Apparently not … but wait, a hand touched his thigh. A grin started until the fingers moved on his right leg. Vicki was on his left. He turned and glared at Jessica. Damn woman. One friggin' drink and she thought they were some sort of item.

He slid his hand beneath the table and covered her hand with his. Jessica shifted beside him, and he lifted her hand off of his thigh and put it on her own before removing his hand.

Jessica made a noise, but Joe ignored her and turned to Vicki, who glared at him before turning her attention back to the president.

"The ElectroTech conference is coming up. I will be sending two of you to the conference, but I'm still in the process of deciding who the two will be. With that said, is there anything else?" No one said anything. "Good. See you all in a month."

Joe pushed back his chair at the same time Vicki did, rising with her. "Lunch?" he whispered.

She started to shake her head. "Victoria, " Mr. Reynolds, the president, called her name. "I have a couple of questions about your marketing report, and Joe, why don't you stay, too? I have some information for you."

The rest of the room filed out. Vicki crossed her arms over her stomach. She didn't have anything to worry about, so why was she so defensive? Joe slipped his hand to the small of her back to guide her to the front of the room, and she jumped.

"Easy, you're good," he whispered.

"You can't know that." She straightened her spine and moved

away from his touch.

Joe frowned. What was going on? He followed her to the front of the room and took a seat next to her.

"Thanks for staying," Reynolds said. "Victoria, I looked over your marketing plan, and I wanted to tell you I'm very impressed."

Her shoulders slumped. Had she'd been worried about her job? That didn't seem right. Joe talked with Michael on a regular basis. Heck, Michael was the one who had encouraged him to work closer with Vicki in some of the marketing aspects of the company.

"Thank you, Mr. Reynolds."

Michael waved away her words. "I wanted you to know how much I appreciated your working this up on short notice on Friday."

So that's why she had been in the building so late. He'd never asked, only thanked his lucky stars they'd been thrown together.

"It wasn't a problem, sir."

The sir stirred Joe's dominant side. Why? Was Vicki into kink? He'd have to ask her, but not on the job.

"I don't like making my employees stay late on Friday night, so I wanted to thank you personally." Vicki nodded, and Michael turned to Joe. "Joe, I wanted to talk to you about the Winnex project."

"You don't need me," Vicki said, rising.

Joe rose to his feet, keeping his gaze on Vicki as she strode from the conference room.

"When I said work with Victoria, I didn't mean you had to get up close and personal," Michael said.

With a laugh, Joe turned back to his friend. "I'll keep it off company time."

"Joe, sexual harassment is a big thing nowadays."

"I promise, Michael, if she says 'no' or 'leave me alone,' I will."

"I believe you." Michael stared at him. "Out of all the people I know, you're the only one I would trust to keep his word. Now, about Winnex."

TWO HOURS LATER, Joe walked to Vicki's department. "Hi, Lisa, is Victoria in her office?"

"Yes, Mr. Bradshaw." She stood.

"I'll let myself in." He waved her back into her chair as he crossed the door to Vicki's office. He knocked before turning the knob.

She glanced up from the computer with a frown on her face. Joe shut the door and sauntered over to her desk.

"What can I do for you, Mr. Bradshaw?"

Now it was his turn to frown. "Joe." He moved around her desk and leaned against the side of it.

She wrinkled her nose at him. "I'm very busy." She returned her attention to her computer screen.

"You have to eat lunch." He took in the way she'd piled her hair up on her head, the stiff way she held her shoulders, and how her gaze darted from her computer screen to him and back.

"I'll have a sandwich at my desk."

"No." He leaned over and captured one of her hands.

Her head snapped up, and her fiery gaze locked onto him. Yes, there was Vicki. "Mr. Bradshaw."

"Each time you call me Mister, I'm going to kiss you. That's twice since I've been in your office."

Her mouth dropped open, and he took advantage of her surprise to stand, push her chair back, and pull her out of it.

"M ... ummm, Joe."

"You're learning." He cradled her close. The scent of honey tickled his nose.

"Joe, we can't." She squirmed in his embrace.

"It's just lunch, Vicki, nothing more."

"But." Her gaze dropped from his.

This wasn't like her. Something was off. "What are you afraid of?"

"We work together, so this is inappropriate."

Joe tilted his head and stared at her. "How? People in this company go out to lunch all the time."

"But they haven't had sex with the other person."

"Who says?" Is that what she was worried about?

"It doesn't matter. I need to get some work done." She squirmed in his hold, but didn't try to get away.

"It's just lunch, nothing special. I want to know you better."

"Do you think you can keep your hands to yourself?"

Joe laughed. "If I have to, but are you saying you don't enjoy my touch?"

"No." Her cheeks turned pink, and then she grinned. "That's not the point."

"It's half the battle." He breathed a sigh of relief. At least she wasn't telling him no or to go away. "I promise I'll be a good boy."

Her grin turned into full laughter. "You were never a good boy." He relaxed his hold, and she slipped from his embrace. "Okay, but to lunch only."

"Fantastic." His heart lightened.

"So, why lunch?" she asked after they were seated at the restaurant.

Joe set his menu down and stared at her. "Why can't we have a simple meal together?"

"Because … " Her voice trailed off and she glanced around the restaurant. "We had sex." Her voice was quiet.

"Yes, and we went out on Saturday, so I don't see the issue." Joe sat back in his chair, keeping his gaze on Vicki. He wanted to know what was going on in her head.

"We work together."

"You've mentioned that. Spit it out. What's bugging you,

Vicki?"

"Favoritism."

He tilted his head. "What could there be? You're marketing, and I'm part of advance creation."

"Implied favoritism." She fiddled with her menu as the waiter arrived. They gave their orders and the waiter left.

"Nothing about our relationship has anything to do with your job or mine. I'm not your boss, and I have no say in your job." Technically it was true; a case could be made, but there was no direct reporting between him and Vicki.

"I know, but others may not." She fiddled with her silverware.

"What aren't you telling me?" There was something—she was too nervous for something minor.

"I ... " She swallowed. "You know I came to TechTronics more than a year ago."

"Yes, you arrived not long before I did."

"I was in a relationship with someone at my last job."

"And?"

"It cost me my job."

Joe swore. He slid his hand across the table and covered her fingers. "That won't happen."

"You can't promise that." The sadness in her eyes tugged at his heart. "I wasn't dating my direct supervisor then, either, but because of the friendship between my supervisor and the guy I was dating, I was fired when the relationship ended."

"That's bullshit. You should sue." Outrage filled him. Yes, he understood sexual harassment laws, but they had been consenting adults, and no one should get fired just because a relationship went sour.

Vicki shook her head. "It was easier to leave." It had been her decision, one she was glad she made. "I don't want to leave TechTronics. I've finally found a job I love."

"What can I do to reassure you?" He wasn't going to give up on her.

"Keep this out of the office." Her gaze grew a bit brighter. "I wouldn't mind going out to dinner, but no more lunches. I want us to be as professional as possible in the office."

She wasn't going to call it off. His heart lightened. "I can do that." The waiter appeared with their food. "Let's eat and then discuss where we're going to dinner."

Vicki laughed. "Give you an inch and you take ten miles."

"With you, I'll take anything I can get."

JOE PULLED UP in front of Vicki's apartment Thursday evening. She was waiting just inside the doors. She hadn't invited him back into her apartment yet. Instead, she met him downstairs each night. Not that he minded.

He watched as she made sure the door to her building was secure behind her. The last few days, he'd found odd notes on the windshield of his car at work. Nothing threatening, but he didn't like it. She had already mentioned an ex. He'd ask her about it, but not tonight.

Shaking off those thoughts, he watched her stroll to his vehicle with a smile on her face.

This week had been a test of his endurance. He left Vicki with a scorching kiss each night, but that was as far as he took it. He was enjoying getting to know her. Tuesday, he had taken her back to Marco's for dinner. They'd talked and he had learned more about her life and her sexual preferences, but nothing that led him to think she was into kink. Wednesday, they'd gone to a play at one of the theaters in Seattle.

Tonight, he was going to surprise her by taking her to the big independent bookstore in downtown Seattle. She'd mentioned how much she loved to read, and he'd seen the books in her apartment.

The car door opened and Vicki slid in. The scent of honey and strawberries tickled his nose. She turned to him, and he leaned over and gave her a quick kiss.

"You smell delicious," he said.

"Thank you." A slight blush crept over her cheeks as she did up her seatbelt. "Where are we going?" she asked as he pulled away from the curb.

"It's a surprise."

She shifted in her seat. "You surprised me last night with tickets to the theater."

"And tonight is another one. Just sit back and relax."

"Easy for you to say."

Joe let out a husky chuckle. The traffic in Seattle had cleared out a bit, so it didn't take them long to get to their destination.

"Oh, Joe." Her face lit up as he escorted her into the bookstore.

"You said you loved reading, so I thought you might like to wander around."

"Yes." Her expression was dreamy as she swiveled her head from side to side, trying to take in everything.

"Go." Joe released her arm and she was off.

He followed her around the store. She was like a kid in a candy shop, stopping to browse the shelves. Fiction, nonfiction, history, romance. Her tastes were as eclectic as the woman herself.

She pulled a couple of books from the history section, looked at them, and re-shelved all but one.

"Let me carry that." He took the book from her.

"Thanks." She moved on to romance.

Within minutes he had ten books. Luckily, he found a basket to carry her books in. But he was enjoying himself because she was so happy. Then she walked into the sexuality section. Joe's interest flared.

Vicki glanced at him, her cheeks flushing, before she turned back to the shelves. Joe maintained his distance, but kept his gaze on what she pulled from the shelves to flip through. First it was a book on new relationships, which she put back after a minute. Then a book about sexual positions.

She began flipping through it, then looked up at him. "Why don't you go look around?"

"I'm fine." Joe grinned at her. "Finding anything interesting?"

Her cheeks turned a deep red, but she didn't put the book back, instead she snapped it shut and dropped it in the basket.

Joe leaned over and whispered in her ear, "I can't wait to try it out with you."

"Behave." She moved away from him.

He couldn't stop smiling until she picked up a book on alternative relationships, this one about threesomes. How interested in kink was she? He scooted closer to her.

"Fantasy or reality?" He kept his voice low even though there was no one else in the section with them.

"Joe," she whispered, putting the book back.

"I can make the fantasy come true if you want."

Vicki turned her head so quickly their noses bumped each other. "Oh, my God, you can't be serious."

"Only if you want." He took her by the arm and guided her over to the far corner. "Are you into kink?"

She bit her lip and lowered her gaze. "And if I am?"

"Then you and I are going to have a very frank talk, because I'd love to get kinky with you."

A giggle left her lips and Joe stared into her gleaming eyes. "I can't wait," she whispered.

His cock jumped behind the fabric of his slacks. Joe glanced around the store; thank goodness there was a small sofa with a table unoccupied close to them. He slipped his arm around her waist and escorted her over to the seating.

"Have a seat and I'll be right back." He set the basket of books on the table, then hurried back to the sexuality section. Scanning the shelves, he pulled off five books and returned to Vicki.

"Let's start with this one." He handed her "Kinky 101" as he sat down next to her.

"Ummm … I've already read it."

"So you know the basics." This was interesting.

"Mostly, yes." While she wasn't totally shy, Joe saw her gaze dart around the store as if to make sure no one was close enough to hear them. She was probably right, this wasn't a conversation for public consumption.

"Have you read any of these books?" He handed her the other four, watching her face as she looked at the titles. Her eyes widened when she got to the flogging book, and her cheeks turned red when she read the bondage title.

The other two books were more basic so he wasn't surprised when she handed him the flogging and bondage books. "Those two I haven't read."

"Good. Let's buy this lot and get out of here."

"I …" She took a deep breath. "I can't buy those books with you standing next to me."

"You won't have to." He helped her stand and tucked the two books under his arm while picking up her basket of books. "I'm buying them for you."

"But won't the clerks put two and two together?" she protested.

"I don't care." He leaned over and touched her forehead with his. "Everyone here will be envious that I have a sexy, adventurous woman with me."

"You always know the right thing to say." Her eyes went dreamy.

"Not always, but I try." He grinned all the way to the checkout. Joe allowed her to go first and buy her purchases. He wanted to buy them for her, but she'd already lectured him on the theater tickets the previous night.

The next cashier opened and Joe paid for his books and met Vicki at the door. Once they were both back in his car, he turned to her.

"Are you willing to be kinky with me?" he asked.

"Define kinky."

Joe thought for a minute. "Toys, bondage, spanking, maybe using a flogger. Beyond the missionary position."

"I want to start off slow."

He nodded. "We will." A plan was already forming in his mind. He knew just the place they could start off slow, yet he could test her kinkiness.

FRIDAY NIGHT, JOE pulled up outside Vicki's apartment building once again. Would she be wearing the dress he had sent her? He knew she had received it because she called him and thanked him for the gift, then proceeded to tell him no more presents.

He loved showering her with small items. "Good evening, Vicki," he said as she climbed into his car, flashing bare legs. Her jacket covered most of her. Did she have the dress on? He'd taken a chance, but when he'd seen it, he couldn't resist. The sleeveless button-down black dress was perfect for her.

"Good evening, Joe." She fastened her seat belt. "Thank you for the beautiful dress. It's a perfect fit, and I don't want to know how you knew what size to get." She grinned at him.

Oh, that grin, that was a teasing Vicki grin. One full of promise and delight. After checking the mirrors, Joe pulled out into traffic. Tonight he had a plan. First stop, Plantation, a small, private restaurant. He'd see how she reacted to it, then he'd go from there.

"Where are we going?" she asked when he drove out of Seattle and headed south.

"Dinner at a place I know." It didn't take them long to reach their destination. He pulled into the small industrial area and parked the car outside a nondescript building.

"Dinner here?" She glanced from him to the building.

"Trust me." He climbed out of the car, then opened her door and helped her out. Keeping their arms linked, he led her to the door where a man stood.

Victoria's curiosity was aroused. Where was Joe taking her? She wondered how there could be a restaurant in this industrial area, but the tantalizing smells of roasting beef teased her nose.

Joe guided her to a door where a burly man stood with a clipboard. Bouncer?

"Joe Bradshaw."

The man looked at the clipboard. "Yes, of course, Mr. Bradshaw." The bouncer slid a key card into the reader, the light flashed green, and an audible click was heard. "Enjoy your evening." The door was pulled open, and Joe escorted her in.

The hallway was dim, but music drifted from the end of the hallway. The music was soft and subtle. They turned the corner, and she stopped in her tracks.

The red-and-white carpet with a flower design brought out the color of the high-backed booths around the outside of the room, with only a few tables in the middle of the floor. Each booth had curtains either pulled back or closed, surrounding them.

"Good evening, Mr. Bradshaw, ma'am." The black-suited maitre d' said, approaching them. "May I take your coat, ma'am?"

She unzipped her coat, slipped it off, and watched Joe from the corner of her eye.

"Oh, shit, I'm in trouble," he whispered.

Victoria hid a smile. The black sleeveless dress fit her to perfection. And the button- down front was something she wouldn't have picked out for herself, but she loved it. The dress flowed over her body perfectly.

The maitre d' cleared his throat after he had handed her coat off to another person. "I have your table ready, if you'll follow me."

Joe gestured for her to follow the man, and she did, adding a little extra hip action to torment him with.

She tried not to stare, but she was so very intrigued by the restaurant. Two of the booths had their curtains drawn as they strode by. The sound of flesh meeting flesh and a giggle made her head turn to one closed-off table; then, as they walked by another, she heard the words, "Yes, suck me, my pet."

What the heck? She tilted her head and stared at Joe, and he grinned and shook his head. But her brain was going a thousand miles an hour as she slid into the booth. Joe followed suit right next to her. "The wine steward will be by shortly with your request."

"Thank you," Joe said, and the maitre d' slipped away.

The booth was bigger than a normal one. While curved and with high backing, the seat was quite wide and very plush. The table had an elegant white tablecloth with a red swirl design on it. Wine glasses, water glasses, silverware, and napkins sat in the middle of the table. A loud moan caused her to jerk her head, and Joe let out a chuckle.

"Interesting place you've brought me to." Her throat was dry.

"The food is worth moaning about."

"Really?" She was suspicious. The other night he had asked her about sexual preferences, and even though she'd played down some of the kinky aspects she enjoyed, she suspected Joe was aware of them. Then last night at the bookstore, Joe had seemed overly interested when she'd browsed around the sexuality section.

Plus they had talked in the car. Her nerves danced against her skin. She wasn't a prude by any means. How could she pretend to be after they'd had sex in the elevator?

But she hadn't exactly been adventurous, either, at least not before their encounter. She hadn't found a man who was interested in a little bit of kink. Yes, she had read about it. Some of it made her cringe, while other parts made her tingle.

"Yes, but there are other things, too." The wine steward arrived, poured a small amount in a glass, and handed it to Joe. She watched as he did the whole wine-tasting thing, then nodded. Wine was poured, water was poured, and then they were left alone.

"Tell me about this place." She took a sip of the red wine.

"Plantation is a very private restaurant." He slid closer to her.

"Like a members only?" Joe's thigh brushed hers, and her entire body heated. What was it about him? It was more than the bad-boy persona. All week, she'd tried to nail down why she was so damn attracted to him.

It hit her at that moment. Joe wasn't afraid of being a man. Wow, that sounded sexist. Her thoughts scattered when he ran his finger over her cheek.

"Sort of. In order to get a reservation here, you must know someone who has a connection with the restaurant."

"And you do?" She swallowed as his fingers caressed her skin, her neck arching as he stroked and petted her.

"The owner." Joe shifted. "He's an old friend."

"You seem to know a lot of restaurant owners."

"Yeah." He grinned. "I enjoy investing in them." He shifted toward her. "Plantation is a restaurant that caters to those who wish to have a nice dinner but also be … shall we say, naughty."

A breathy moan escaped her lips as his fingers dipped to the base of her neck, then toyed with the first button of her dress, undoing it so he could tease the valley between her breasts.

"Sexy naughty?" she whispered.

"Yes." His breath teased her ear. "Remember what you heard walking by the closed curtain booths?"

She nodded and words caught in her throat. He couldn't mean …

"Good evening." A male voice interrupted them. "So sorry to interrupt, Mr. Bradshaw, but the chef wanted me to inform you your entree would be ready in about thirty minutes. Would you like your salad now?"

Victoria closed her eyes and took a breath as Joe removed his hand and spoke to the waiter. Her blood was tingling along with other parts of her body. Her nipples were tight.

"That's fine." The waiter scurried away, and Joe's attention turned back to her. "So, where was I? Oh, yes, the closed booths."

"You can't mean they were … " She shook her head.

"Yes." His warm palm cupped her chin. "The first I'm pretty sure was a very nice spanking, the second was pretty self-explanatory."

"But." She glanced around the restaurant. It was almost a full house. "Does everyone … indulge?"

"Not everyone," he whispered. "But many find it a thrill." He fingered the second button on her dress.

"Do you?" She swallowed.

"Depends." The button loosened under his ministrations.

Victoria held her breath, but the second button didn't reveal much. The slight swell of her breasts was all. But a shot of excitement flowed through her veins. "Ummm."

The clearing of a throat snapped her from Joe's heated gaze. The waiter's face was impassive; it would have to be, working here.

"Excuse me, your salad." He set the large salad on the table in front of Joe. "I'll be back with your main course when it's ready."

"There's only one salad," she said after the waiter walked

away.

"Yes." Joe picked up a set of silverware and an extra napkin. Opening the napkin, he laid it in her lap. Then he unwrapped the silverware and put a napkin in his lap. "You see," he said as he lifted the fork, "with only one salad, I get to feed you." He speared some lettuce and held it to her lips.

She opened her mouth and let him slip the food inside. After she chewed and swallowed, she licked her lips. A fire lit in Joe's blue eyes. Placing her hand on the table, she inched her way over to the silverware, snagged a fork, and held it up.

"My turn." She lifted the food-filled fork to his mouth. A shiver went through her body as he closed his lips over the food. They continued to feed each other until the salad was gone.

Her skin was flushed and tight by the time their main meal arrived. Again, only one plate. A huge plate at that. The scent of roasted beef and butter made her mouth water.

"Would you please pull the curtain?" Joe requested of the waiter.

"Of course, sir. Just signal when you're ready for me to remove the plate or if you need anything." Within minutes the curtain was released and encased their table.

Her breath caught in her throat. What was Joe going to do?

"That's better." He cupped her neck and brushed a light kiss over her lips. "Now we can enjoy ourselves." He flicked open the third button on her dress, revealing her lacy bra.

Victoria wiggled in her seat. Could she do this? Who was she trying to kid? She felt anticipation along with a healthy dose of keen awareness that they could get caught. But who would catch them? The waiter had already said he wouldn't come back until signaled.

"Okay?" Joe asked, his fingers hovering over the next button.

She nodded and the fourth button was opened.

"So beautiful," Joe whispered before turning to their meal. He cut the large piece of meat, then fed her a bite.

The beef flavor exploded along with Italian spices over her tongue. She moaned.

Joe didn't think his cock could get any harder, but Vicki's moan proved him wrong. His lady was more than ready for anything he could throw at her. After they had fed each other more food, he undid a couple more buttons of her dress.

Now it was open to below her waist. Dipping his index finger in his wine, he trailed it between her breasts. She leaned her head back, and he licked the wine from her skin.

"So sweet," he murmured against her skin.

Her fingers tangled in his hair as he cupped her breast through the lace while nuzzling between her globes. Shifting in the booth, he slid his right arm behind her neck.

"You've been driving me crazy."

"I don't mean to." Her throaty response heated his blood.

"I know, but you are so sexy, so beautiful, and so responsive." The silverware rattled as he pushed the table away with his foot. "If you want me to stop, say Red."

"Yes, Sir," she whispered.

Every nerve in his body went on alert at her words. Lifting his head from between her breasts, he took her lips in a hard kiss as he unbuttoned more of her dress, only breaking the kiss so he could reach the last two buttons.

Once the dress was undone, he spread it apart, revealing her black lacy bra and panties. Her nipples were poking against the fabric. Thank goodness it was a front-clasp bra. He unsnapped the clasp.

Her hands rose, but one was trapped by his body; the other he grasped by her wrist. "I want to see you, taste you."

Her arm relaxed, and he released her wrist. "Good girl." He nuzzled her breast before taking one nipple in his mouth while his other hand pinched the other nipple.

Another moan escaped her lips, and she arched into his mouth and touch. Damn, she was responsive. He switched to her other breast while his hand slid down her stomach to her thighs.

She clenched her legs together, and he bit her nipple lightly before letting it slip from his lips. "Open your legs, sweetheart."

"I … " Slowly her legs parted.

"That's it." He captured her nipple once again as his fingers tunneled under the elastic of her panties until he parted her nether lips. "So wet," he whispered.

Her body trembled as he kissed his way down to her stomach, his right hand sliding down her arm. He pushed his finger into her channel, and she let out a mewing sound.

"Not too loud," he whispered.

"Oh, my God," was all she said as he pressed a second finger into her.

She was deliciously responsive, and he slid in a third finger.

"Joe … Sir." Her breathless voice sent a shaft of lust through him.

"You're so wet, so willing." He pressed his thumb against her clit, and she bucked against his hand. He continued to pump his fingers in and out of her pussy while his thumb tormented her clit.

Her legs began to shake, and her muscles clamped around his fingers. She was close. "Come for me, sweetheart."

"I … I … "

"But do it quietly unless you want everyone to know." He glanced up at her flushed face in time to see her clamp her jaw shut; her body grew rigid as she exploded. God, he wanted to take her right then and there, but he wouldn't. This was for her, for her to know and understand what they did as consenting adults was for them.

Her spine relaxed, and she slumped in her seat. Joe slipped

his fingers from her wetness. Her lips parted as she tried to catch her breath.

"So fucking gorgeous." His lips covered hers in a soft kiss before he sat back. His cock throbbed with unfulfilled desire, but her soft breaths of pleasure were more than enough, for now.

He licked her juices from his fingers, enjoying her spiciness. When he glanced over at her she was watching him with desire in her eyes.

"You are a wicked, bad boy."

He chuckled. "You have no idea." He leaned over and brushed a kiss over her lips. "Dessert?"

"I think someone already had his." Her eyes sparkled, and all he could do was laugh.

Victoria refastened her bra and then buttoned up her dress. Part of her was mortified she'd let Joe bring her to a climax in the restaurant, but the other part relished his reaction to her.

Joe lifted his hand and seconds later the curtains rustled, then parted. Their waiter stood there. "Dessert? Coffee?" he asked as he picked up the plate and their silverware.

"Two coffees, please," Joe said.

With a nod, their waiter disappeared and the curtain fell back into place. "So do you come here a lot?" She pressed her lips together; that wasn't the question she'd meant to ask.

"No." His fingers curved around her neck, stroking her skin in a gentle caress. "You're the first woman I've brought here."

"Okay." She flashed him a grin, but squirmed in her seat as he leaned closer.

"Are you embarrassed?"

"A bit." She glanced up at him. "You made me orgasm in a restaurant full of people."

"And most were doing the same thing." His lips caressed her ear. "Stop and really listen for a moment."

She closed her eyes and did as he said. Yes, there was the clatter of plates and cutlery, the music was still playing, and … then she heard several soft moans, a sigh, and then a small cry.

"You're not alone in your pleasure tonight, sweetheart. Passion is nothing to be embarrassed about."

Victoria nodded, then took a deep breath. "How kinky are you?" she blurted out in a rush.

His fingers tightened on her neck. "Depends on what you like."

"I'm not sure." And she wasn't. But dang if she wasn't getting wet again thinking about Joe making her climax with his fingers where anyone could hear them.

"Then we'll explore together."

The curtains parted, and the waiter arrived with their coffee.

VICTORIA WOKE SATURDAY morning to bright sunshine. Ah, the Pacific Northwest weather could be so unpredictable. She stretched and then climbed out of bed. She glanced over at the clock. Nine. Joe had said he would be here at eleven to pick her up.

Another one of his surprises. Victoria smiled as she wandered into the bathroom. Joe was being mysterious but very attentive. She hugged herself. It was nice to have a man who cared about her satisfaction and her life.

She took a quick shower and pulled her hair into a ponytail. Joe had told her to dress casually. After feeding her cat, she made coffee and some toast and let her memory of last night fill her.

They'd been so naughty at the restaurant. Actually, Joe was the one who'd been naughty, she had just let him bring her to orgasm. Heat slid over her face. She was still having trouble with how Joe made her climax last night. Anyone could have heard her.

But wasn't that the point? She absently buttered her toast and took it out to the table. Plantation was all about the thrill of doing something sexual in public. Victoria didn't consider herself an exhibitionist, but dang if Joe couldn't turn her on faster than flicking a light switch.

Was that a bad thing? She paused to consider the question. How did she really feel about Joe? She liked him, she trusted him. How strange she'd forged a bond with him so quickly. Or was it? She'd seen him over a year ago, and he revved her engines then. Now they were constantly humming. She let out a giggle.

Her cell beeped, so she picked it up and stared at the screen. It was Joe sending her a text message.

Joe: On my way

Her: I'm ready and willing

Now why did she type that? Talk about your unconscious self being revealed.

Joe: Are you trying to kill me, woman?

Her: No, I want you very much alive.

Joe: Good. Wait until I get you alone.

She set her phone down, anticipation tingling through her body. She enjoyed bantering with Joe. She hadn't had that with Derek. Banishing all thoughts of Derek, she cleaned up her breakfast dishes.

Twenty minutes later her doorbell rang. She skipped over to the door, looked out the peephole, and then unlocked the door.

"Good morning," she said with a bright smile.

"Morning." The words barely left his mouth before he dropped the bag he was carrying, hauled her into his arms, and covered her mouth with his.

Victoria sighed into the kiss. His lips were cool, but firm. His hold was gentle compared to his lips plundering hers. When he lifted his head they were both breathing hard.

"Wow," she breathed out the word.

"That's what you get for teasing me."

"Is that what I was doing?" She turned to pick up her purse, but glanced over her shoulder at him.

Joe let out a growl and she fought against smiling. "Where are we off to?"

"I'm not telling you, but you'll need to wear this." He picked up the bag from where he dropped it and pulled out a leather jacket.

"Joe?" The leather gleamed in the muted morning light.

"Come on, we don't have all day." He held the jacket for her.

This time she laughed. "Impatient." She slipped one arm into the supple leather, then the other. It fit. "How did you know my size?"

"I know lots of things." He drew a finger down her nose. "Let's go." He shifted from one foot to the other as she locked up her apartment, then took her hand as they took the elevator down to the lobby.

Outside the front door stood a gleaming, massive motorcycle. "Oh, my God, you're going to give me a ride on your motorcycle." She practically bounced with excitement. She'd always wanted to ride one.

For the first time she noticed what he was wearing. A leather jacket, with black jeans and leather boots. "I guess it's a good thing I have on jeans."

"Helmet." He reached for the black helmet sitting on the seat when she noticed a white paper.

"Oh no, did you get a ticket?"

Joe plucked the paper off the seat. "No worries." He folded it and shoved it into his pocket. He slid a helmet onto her head and adjusted it. "It's fully wired so we can talk to each other as we ride."

Victoria nodded. Joe slipped his black helmet on and mounted the bike. "Get on behind me. Feet on the foot rests, and arms around my waist."

She eyed the bike. Think of it as a horse, just throw your leg over. Victoria took a deep breath, swung her left leg up and over the seat, then grabbed Joe's shoulders as the motorcycle wobbled.

"Good mount. Do you see where to place your feet?"

"Got it." She placed her feet on the metal tabs, and then slid her arms down Joe's back and around his waist.

The bike flared to life. The vibrations from the motor sent a ripple of tremors to her pussy.

"Ready?" Joe looked over his shoulder at her.

"As I'll ever be."

Victoria let out a small squeak as Joe pulled out into traffic. She admired how he kept a good distance between them and other vehicles, never driving too fast or too slow.

"How are you doing?" he asked.

"Great." While the wind tugged at her clothing, it helped her understand the freedom.

"In a few minutes, we'll be outside city limits and I'm going to go faster. If it bothers you, let me know."

"Okay." When Joe turned onto another road, the vibrations beneath her changed. Her arms automatically tightened around his waist and he sped up. Her heart pounded. Now she understood the freedom people got from being on a motorcycle.

All too soon he was slowing down, guiding the bike up a winding road. As they arrived at the top, Joe shifted and the gate opened. Her eyes widened as he drove the bike up the circular driveway and stopped in front of a white two-story home.

The rumbling of the motorcycle stopped; Victoria released her hold on Joe and stared at the building. "You brought me to your house?"

"Yes." Somehow Joe managed to slip off the motorcycle with her still sitting on the back. He then helped her dismount and removed her helmet. "Welcome to my home."

Victoria did a slow turn, taking in the beautiful stone

pathways, the towering pine trees, and the subtle hint of jasmine.

"It's beautiful." Her stomach tightened. Why had he brought her here? Yes, he'd seen and been inside her apartment, but she didn't expect to see his home.

"Come on." He took her hand in his and led her up the path, then he unlocked the door. "Let me get the alarm." Joe slipped inside, then held his hand out to her.

Her breath caught in her throat. The entry hall was huge, and there was a large hardwood staircase leading to the second floor. "How do you keep it so clean?"

Joe stared at her and Victoria burst out laughing. "Sorry, it was the first thing that popped into my head."

"I have a housekeeper who comes in once a week." He shut the front door. "Come on, I'll give you the nickel tour."

"Why such a large house?" she asked.

"I wanted a place where I had room to grow."

Victoria wrinkled her nose at him, but didn't say more. Was he thinking of something more permanent with her? More than just a fling? It was obvious to her he'd bought the home for a future wife and kids.

"And for the crowning glory." He grinned as he led her into the backyard.

"Oh, my." An Olympic-size pool graced the backyard.

"As you see, the pool, and down that pathway," he gestured to his right, "are the tennis courts."

"Wow, Joe. This is amazing."

"I'm glad you like it." He leaned toward her. "Let's go skinny-dipping."

"I ... " She closed her eyes and bit her lower lip. Deep inside of her, she wanted to strip off her clothes and skinny-dip with him. But she'd never been that daring, that bold. Except the night in the elevator.

"Breathe, sweetheart." His warm breath tickled her skin. "We can do that at a later date when you're more comfortable with me. For now, let me make us lunch."

Victoria took a deep breath and followed Joe back into the house. One small crisis averted. She would have to watch her step around him, because she was falling under his spell.

Chapter Five

Monday morning, Victoria sat in her office staring out the window. After spending Saturday with Joe she'd been floating until she listened to the messages on her machine.

Derek.

She'd had enough. Sunday morning, she called the police department and went down and talked to an officer. They took a report, listened to her recordings, and told her they would do what they could. She did have the option of taking out a restraining order on Derek, so she started the paperwork to get that done.

It was time to get Derek out of her life. The last officer she'd spoken with suggested the next time Derek called for her to answer the phone and explain if he continued the police would get involved. He also suggested she change her phone number one more time. They would also, at her request, send a copy of the police report to the phone company to trace the calls if Derek continued. She agreed with the officer to follow up. Hopefully, now she'd made the legal filing, Derek would get the message. She was so done with this chapter of her life.

Her phone buzzed. She turned away from the window and hit the speaker. "Yes, Lisa."

"You're wanted upstairs." Her secretary's voice came across the intercom.

"Upstairs?" Victoria blinked. Had Joe demanded her presence? She grew wet. Oh, God, she had to stop this.

"Mr. Reynolds called and asked if you could come up."

What did Mr. Reynolds want? "Thanks, Lisa." Victoria blew out a breath before standing. Did he have a question about her marketing plan? She printed off another copy and put it in a file to take with her before marching out of her office.

Stepping into the elevator, she'd swear she could still smell the scent of her erotic coupling with Joe. She breathed a sigh of relief when she arrived on the twenty-first floor, where Mr. Reynolds' office was, without stopping.

Carla, his executive assistant, smiled when Victoria entered the office. "Hi, Victoria. He's waiting for you. Go on in."

"Thanks, Carla. How's the baby?" Carla's baby girl had been diagnosed with a case of colic. Being a first time mother, she had panicked.

"Sally's much better. Thanks for asking."

"You're welcome." Victoria strode over to the door, knocked, and entered when she heard the gruff "Come in."

JOE'S GAZE CLASHED with Vicki's, and he sucked in a breath. Back was the prim and proper Victoria, but it didn't stop his pulse from racing or his cock from stiffening. What was she wearing beneath her stuffy, plain business outfit today? Did she have on another lacy camisole and her garters? Was she wearing silk panties? A thong? Or nothing at all? His fingers itched to find out. Later.

"Ah, Victoria, thank you for coming right away." Michael Reynolds stood and smiled at her.

Joe rose to his feet. He had to give her credit; only the slight widening of her eyes gave away her surprise at seeing him there.

Well, if she thought he was going to disappear at work, she was dead wrong.

"Please, sit down." Michael waved at the empty chair next to Joe.

With a wary glance, she moved forward and sat. Joe slid his chair closer to hers before sitting. Her gaze flickered to his face, but this time he could see real unease in those green eyes before she snapped her gaze away. Was she still embarrassed over their time in the elevator? Or Friday night at the restaurant? Saturday at his home? Nervous about why she was called up to Reynolds' office? Or was there something else going on?

"Did you have a question about the new marketing report, Mr. Reynolds?" she asked with a small tremor in her voice.

Was she nervous or scared? He wanted to reach out and take her hand in reassurance, but knew he couldn't do that, not with another person in the room. He had to be all business, but when they were alone—well, it would be a different matter altogether.

"No. The report is fine. Joe needs your help."

Her spine stiffened. "My help?"

A delicate eyebrow rose, and Joe stifled a chuckle. She looked so sexy when she was suspicious.

"I don't understand," she continued.

Joe turned in his chair, his knee bumping hers. She pulled her leg back at the contact. Not a good sign. His Vicki was hiding once again. Or could she be scared of him? Mentally he shook his head. His Vicki wasn't frightened of anything. But wait a minute—he remembered the momentary fear in her gaze when she looked at the crowd when they were out at Shilshole Bay. He needed to find out more about the guy who had her looking over her shoulder. Plus there were those odd notes he kept getting.

"I need someone to attend the ElectroTech conference with me. Our plane leaves in three hours," Joe said.

"But … " Her fingers tightened around the folder and notebook, her eyes narrowing and her teeth sinking into her lower lip. His cock jumped.

Reynolds grimaced as he placed his hands on his desk. "I know this is short notice, Victoria. Henry was planning to go, but his wife went into early labor, and you were next on the list. Your marketing expertise will be invaluable. You'll be very well compensated."

"My marketing expertise?" Her tone was icy.

Joe watched her closely. Something wasn't right here. Why was she so suspicious? Hadn't they gotten past this yet? "You have a degree in marketing."

"True, but … Mr. Reynolds," she started, looking at Michael rather than Joe, "it isn't about the money. It's just—I couldn't leave town on such short notice."

"Has something changed in your life?" Reynolds looked at her with a frown. "Last time we talked, you were single with no family."

"Um, no." She swallowed.

"Michael, I'm sure what Ms. Collins is trying to say is three hours is barely enough time to pack and find someone to babysit her cat."

Her gaze snapped back to his face, and this time he didn't stop the grin forming on his lips. He had surprised her. Good. He wanted to keep her on her toes around him.

She nodded.

"If you can't find anyone, let me know. I'll have Carla make arrangements for you." Reynolds stared at her with an intense expression. "Your only objection, right?"

Her knuckles turned white as she clenched her hands. What else could she say? She wouldn't mention what happened between them in the elevator or on their date in front of Michael.

"Yes." Her voice was tight and controlled.

"Good." Michael stood. "Joe, I know you'll do a good job."

"I'll do my best." He cupped Victoria's elbow to escort her from the room.

She glared at him but didn't pull away. He didn't expect her to make a scene. Vicki might take him to task, but she wouldn't make a scene. He studied her, trying to figure out why she was so uptight at work. Together they walked past Carla to the elevators.

His body tightened at the thought of being in an elevator with her again. After going out all last week with her, his fantasies still centered around their Friday night encounter at the Plantation. Even masturbating hadn't helped. He was still hard. If the trip provided him an opportunity to get her into bed again, he would, but only if she was willing.

The bell pinged and the elevator doors opened. With precise movements, Joe ushered her in and pressed the button for the seventeenth floor. The doors closed and the car began to descend.

"How dare you?" She pulled away from him, her spine stiff, her green eyes shooting fire, the folder pressed against her chest.

"What did I do?" He raised his hands in mock surrender. God, she was beautiful, especially when she was angry. Cliché or not, it was the truth, but he would have loved to see her happy rather than angry.

"You know darn well—" She broke off when the elevator stopped.

Several people entered, and she moved to the right front corner. Joe followed, ignoring her scathing gaze. When the doors opened on the seventeenth floor, he held them, gesturing for her to precede him.

Fire brewed in her eyes as she glared at him before she strode out of the elevator with her head held high. He trailed behind, enjoying the way her bottom moved in the black skirt. As they neared his office, he grasped her arm, pulling her to a halt. "Are you wearing garters again?" he whispered.

Her lashes fell, and she didn't answer. Not knowing only increased the hardness of his cock. He opened the door to his office and gestured for her to enter.

"I don't think … " she started, as apprehension flickered in her eyes.

While he wasn't surprised by her reluctance, he wasn't going to let her go, either. He needed to get to the bottom of why she was so upset. "Please," he said in a soft tone. "I promise I won't bite."

She rolled her eyes and marched past him.

"At least not at this moment," he commented as he tailed her into his office. He shut the door and engaged the lock. They really didn't have time for this, but he wanted to reassure her that she held all the cards on this trip. He would respect her space if she told him so.

If Victoria asked to leave, he'd let her. His control around her wasn't in top form. The last thing he wanted was someone walking in when he was in the midst of losing it, so he locked the door. He'd worked in the corporate world long enough to know sexual acting-out wasn't tolerated in most companies.

Joe wanted to be with her, to spend time with her, and if the only way he could get close to her was in a platonic work situation, he would. But after hours, he wanted her to agree to no restrictions. She would be all his, the way he wanted her, any way he wanted her. He hoped to win her over to his way of thinking. He was going to woo her, seduce her onto his side.

"Let's get something straight, Mr. Bradshaw." She slapped the folder on the table and then whirled around and faced him.

The passion in her eyes caused fire to stream through his veins. He wanted her passion. Her fire. Just her. "We are at work, no more shenanigans," she declared, poking him in the chest with her finger.

He placed a hand over his heart and stepped back. "You wound me, fair lady." He wiggled his eyebrows.

"Oh, cut the bullshit." She placed her hands on her hips. She glared at him, looking a bit like a Norse goddess of war.

"There is no bullshit here." He spread his arms wide, allowing the grin he was fighting to sneak across his lips. There was his Vicki. The fiery, sexy woman he wanted to fuck day and night; the woman he wanted to make his life exciting rather than dull. "I told you Saturday you were going to set the pace."

His grin seemed to infuriate her even more. Her fingers clenched and her back stiffened further. "Don't give me that sexy, devilish grin of yours. I won't—"

"So you think I'm sexy." He rubbed his chin, unable to stop his grin growing.

"No, I don't."

"You said sexy, devilish grin. I kind of like it." He moved forward.

"You would." She threw her arms up. "This isn't getting us anywhere."

Had he read her wrong? No, he knew the passionate woman beneath the cool façade. "What is it, Vicki? What's got you so upset?"

She turned away from him, her spine rigid, her arms wrapped around her waist in protection. From him? His gut clenched and he slid to her side, wanting to embrace and comfort her, to tell her he'd protect her. But he held back. Something was eating at her, and he wanted to know what it was.

"Vicki?"

"It was too fast," she whispered, gazing at him. Her eyes were clouded with pain. "Everything is happening too fast. I'm not sure what's going on. Not only with my body, but my mind. I'm in a damn tailspin. And I still want you."

For a moment, pure unadulterated relief flooded him. She still wanted him. "We're attracted to each other." Understatement of the year, but the truth. And he also understood he had to take part of the blame for pushing her on Friday. "I'll admit I came on a little strong."

"A little?" Her right eyebrow quirked up.

"Okay. I've got a dominant personality." He shrugged.

She let out a laugh. "I feel like I've been flattened by a steamroller."

"Not my intention," he lied. He wanted to keep her captive in his bedroom, but he also realized something or someone had sent her into hiding. He hated that something bad had happened to her, and he vowed to make her his number one priority. Without conscious thought, he ran his finger down her cheek.

She sucked in a breath. "I don't know if I can trust myself to be alone with you."

Yes! "That's what I want." He forced himself not to pump his fist in the air in triumph. She was his sexually; now he'd make her his emotionally. "I want the uncontrolled woman."

"But that's not me." The panic in her voice made him realize she was fighting against Vicki with every fiber of her being. Again, he wondered why.

"It is you." He took a step. "There's a very passionate, sexy Vicki hiding beneath the prim and proper Victoria. I don't know what happened to make you suppress her, and I'm willing to wait until you're ready to tell me, but don't shut me—or her—out." He might not push her for an answer, but he wasn't going to let her hide. If he let her get away with it, then she'd never open up to him, and he wasn't going to allow that to happen.

"And if I'm never ready to tell you?" she asked, sadness

creeping into her voice.

"I'll deal with it." And he would, if it came to that point. But something told him once she stopped fighting, she'd tell him the whole story. Her shoulders dropped. "I've never taken another woman to Plantation. You responded in such an honest, positive manner, I could barely see straight." Let's see if he could hurry the process a bit. He was never a patient man.

Her cheeks flushed. "You were so demanding."

"And that frightened you?"

She shook her head. "Turned me on."

"And Saturday?"

Her lips turned up. "It was fun and different."

"Then why so doubtful now? What's the worst possible scenario?" He put his hands on her waist, pulling her toward him.

"I could lose my job again." She clamped a hand over her mouth. She hadn't meant to blurt that out a second time. But he was glad she had. He didn't want her worrying about her job.

He wanted all her fears revealed so they could deal with them and heal her. He wanted a future with her. "Your job has nothing to do with what's between us."

"It won't matter." She tried to pull away, but he tightened his hold on her.

He hated the sadness in her voice, the belief if she gave in to what she was feeling, she'd be the loser. "I promised you to keep our relationship separate from work. And I will do that. Outside the workplace will be a different matter."

"And what about today?" She bit her lower lip, making his stomach tighten with the need to soothe the marks with his tongue.

"Reynolds asked me if I had any objection to your going to the conference with me. I don't."

"So it wasn't your idea?"

"No, it was all his." He framed her face with his palms. "Let's explore what's happening between us. Let me take the lead and take care of you. I promise I won't let you down. And if you say no, I'll back away. No questions asked." He scrutinized the flitter of emotions through her sea-green eyes. Fear, excitement, wariness … and then acceptance. The knot in his stomach loosened.

"All right," she whispered, her lips turning up into a small grin.

The relief almost brought him to his knees. He didn't know what he would've done if she hadn't agreed. Probably something totally unacceptable for the workplace, and he would have lost her forever.

"Work starts in ten minutes," he said, as he slid his hands from her waist to her neck, cradling it between his palms.

"Ten minutes?"

"Yes. First, I need something to tide me over until we're off duty." He lowered his head, brushing his lips against hers, then pulled back. He wanted more than just a brief taste, but he wasn't going to abuse her trust. He'd keep it light and easy for now.

"Oh, Joe." She leaned forward and their lips met once again briefly before parting. Her expression was dreamy. "I need more."

"One deep, wet kiss, and then we're all business." He wanted her agreement before he proceeded. "No more misunderstandings."

"Shut up and kiss me."

He chuckled and captured her mouth. Her lips parted, allowing him to thrust his tongue inside, tangling with hers. And she gave back as good as she got. As her arms curved around his neck, he let his hands slide from her face past her shoulders to settle around her hips, cradling her to him. Once he broke the kiss, he trailed his lips to her ear. "I want to strip you, spread you out on my desk, and sink my cock into your hot, moist pussy."

Her breath ruffled his hair as she let out a shaky sigh and trembled in his arms.

"Think about it, my cock sinking into your softness. Your mewling cries as I make you climax, not once, not twice, but three times." He couldn't wait to feel her contract around his dick once again.

"You're not playing fair," she whispered.

"I play to win." His lips seized hers again, his tongue mimicking what he wanted to do with his body. This time, she broke the kiss. He found her earlobe and nipped it, before soothing it with his tongue. His body was hard and on alert. Her breathing was uneven, and a flash of pleasure flowed through him at being able to arouse her so easily. "You'll come with me."

"Oh, yes. Make me come, Joe." Her words were soft and pleading.

He gave a chuckle. "I meant you'll attend the conference with me." He needed confirmation she was okay with the trip.

She leaned back in his embrace, and their gazes met, the dreamy expression on her face clearing. "Oh." She glanced away as her face turned pink. She studied the wall.

"Think about it." He kept his hands around her waist. "Long nights together in bed, in the shower, on the floor, against the wall, wherever it suits us to make love. My hands on your body, in your pussy, playing with your nipples, my cock thrusting into your wetness, your heat." He pressed his hips forward as his hands cupped her ass, molding his palms against her, holding her in place. "Think of the kinky fun we can have."

Her eyes flared with passion, want, and need before her lashes lowered, cutting him off. "Joe," she started. "I don't think—"

"Don't overthink it. Let's explore our attraction to each other. I'm not asking for a lifetime." At least not yet. He'd give her time to get used to their being in a relationship.

"I didn't think you were." Her gaze lifted, her eyes bright. "You're not a man who'd settle for one woman."

A flash of annoyance slipped through him. "You shouldn't listen to gossip." He dropped a kiss on her nose. "Yes, I like women, but I never get involved with more than one at a time. I promise." Her body softened in his arms, and he exploited it. "How would you explain to the boss why you're not willing to go to the conference with me?" He was pulling out the big gun. "Come with me, Vicki. You want to. I know you do. Take a chance. I promise you won't regret it."

Her chest rose as she took a deep breath. Before she could answer him, a knock sounded at the door.

Joe smothered a growl of annoyance. "We'll continue this later." He released her and quietly unlocked the door, throwing it open. His secretary, Sandra, stood there with an apologetic look on her face.

"Sorry to bother you, Mr. Bradshaw, but Mr. Reynolds just called about the figures you gave him this morning, and since you're leaving soon … "

Joe waved aside the rest of her words. "That's okay, Sandra. Ms. Collins and I were just strategizing about what we need to accomplish during the trip."

"Yes, we were." Vicki's voice was cool, and if he didn't know better, he would have thought ice ran through her veins.

"Out front in ten minutes," he told her. "A taxi will be waiting for us."

"But my car is here." Her tone was all business.

"So is mine. They'll be fine in the parking garage."

She nodded and strode out of his office past his secretary.

Joe watched her, admiration coursing through his veins. He might want a woman who was submissive, but damn, he loved it when Vicki fought him, arousing him beyond belief. She wouldn't be a pushover, and he didn't want one. He wanted a woman who'd challenge him, and she was perfect. He wouldn't pressure her if she became frightened. He'd get to the bottom of the past man in her life who made her afraid, but their relationship was going to happen; he refused to let her suppress the woman within or deny what was between them. He rubbed his hands together in anticipation.

VICTORIA TOOK THE stairs back to the third floor. Stopping on the fifth-floor landing, she pulled in a deep breath and let it out with fierce concentration. What the heck had she just done? Giving in to his seductive voice and a promise he couldn't possibly keep!

How could she have let Joe overwhelm her good sense? Easily. All her rational thoughts and actions fled when she was near him. She hated he could affect her so physically, but she couldn't seem to stop the tightening of her nipples or the way her pussy gushed when he was near. It was even worse since they'd had sex. Only once, and she wanted to be in his arms more than ever.

But this was her job he was playing with. While she could find other employment, she didn't want to. She loved her job, and outside of some long hours when things got hectic, the benefits were good and the pay wasn't bad. Then there was Derek, the mental and emotional turmoil she had to overcome because of her involvement with him, although she was slowly recovering from the crap Derek had caused.

Starting at the sound of a door slamming, she moved down the rest of the stairs and back to her office. Oh, shit. The bitchy secretarial manager, Jessica Neimier, was standing next to her desk, arms folded across her ample chest and foot tapping against the carpet. What did Jessica want now? Vicki glanced at Lisa, who mouthed a silent "I'm sorry."

"There you are." Her tone was accusing, as if Victoria were a child who had run off without permission.

"What can I do for you?" Victoria forced herself to speak as normally as she could and not let her annoyance show. Lisa would be able to hear every word, so Victoria needed to keep this professional. There were some days she wanted to take Jessica down a peg or two.

"I understand you're going to accompany Joe to the ElectroTech conference." Disbelief tinged Jessica's voice.

"Good news travels fast," Victoria muttered, striding over to her desk. If she didn't go now, everyone would wonder why she had refused. Not that she was planning on refusing; the picture Joe painted still dominated her thoughts. But damn it, she hated being backed into a corner.

"Wanted to let you know that Joe called me to say goodbye."

"Really?" Had Joe lied to her when he said he wasn't involved with anyone? Why couldn't she pick a man who was honest with her? Wait a second. Joe had said he was never involved with more than one woman at a time. She wanted to believe him. With Jessica here confronting her, the office gossips were going to have a field day. Clearly, Jessica didn't know the meaning of the word discretion. Victoria turned to retrieve her jacket.

"It seems to me," the bitch continued in a snide, condescending voice, "you've been playing a game. Who would've thought a mousy thing," Jessica's lip curled in a sneer before she continued, "like you would have the nerve to sleep with Joe Bradshaw? I believe I underestimated you, but remember—I had him first, so don't think you're special."

"Victoria *is* very special," a familiar male voice said.

Victoria spun around. Her heart clenched. "J— Mr. Bradshaw," Victoria stammered.

"Ms. Neimier," Joe began, and Victoria shivered at the iciness in his blue gaze and voice. "Let me set the record straight." His words were clipped. "You and I have never had a relationship, nor have I ever expressed interest in you."

Victoria almost felt sorry for Jessica when her face turned red with embarrassment, but the woman deserved it. "I never meant to—"

Joe cut off her words with an impatient wave of his hand. "Clear?"

"Yes, Mr. Bradshaw," Jessica mumbled.

"Good. You're free to leave." He turned to Victoria. "Are you ready?"

Chapter Six

Joe noticed the pain in Vicki's eyes from Jessica Neimier's words, and he silently cursed the woman. One after-work drink with Jessica and she'd built up a lie to taunt others with. "Vicki," he started.

She shook her head and marched out of her office, stopping to talk with her secretary before leaving, not even looking back to see if he were following.

Damn it! He was making progress with Vicki, and Neimier had to mess it up. He shook his head in disbelief as he quickened his pace to catch Vicki, barely making it to the elevator before the doors closed.

"You don't understand, do you?" There was pain and exasperation in her voice.

"I guess I don't." The elevator ground to a halt and the doors opened. He cupped her elbow in his palm and escorted her through the lobby, out the double glass doors and to the waiting taxi he'd called the second she'd left his office.

"Joe, you can let go of me."

"And let you run?" He'd seen the fight-or-flight response in her gaze.

"I won't. Please let me go." Her voice was soft.

He stared down into her green eyes. They were clouded with unhappiness, and he needed to back off once again, or he was going to lose her. "Okay." Joe released her arm, and she slid into the waiting cab. He didn't know what the hell was going on; he only knew some man had hurt her, and it had been someone she worked with. He hated being at a loss about how to fix things.

He needed to watch his step, especially if he didn't want her bolting on him. *Take it slow.* Take only what she's willing to give, and don't push. But it wasn't easy for him to take it slow. He wanted her like he wanted no other woman, and the taste of her filled every one of his senses. She was a challenge, one he relished.

Joe handed his duffle bag to the cabbie, and then climbed into the cab after her. As soon as the driver got behind the wheel, he told him Vicki's address. The second he shut the door, the cab shot forward. Vicki was thrown sideways toward the door. Joe reached out to help her, but she stiffened at his touch. Back to square one. "Talk about it," he said. Better to get things out in the open.

"About what?" She threw her hands in the air, just missing hitting him on the nose. "About the fact my reputation in the office is shot to hell because everyone thinks I'm another one of your playmates?" Her voice was low and tight.

His brain picked out one word. "Playmates? What the hell are you talking about?"

"Figures. Men are always so damn clueless." She turned her face away, staring out the window.

"Yes, we are." And he was clueless. He didn't have any idea of what she was talking about. "What's going on inside that amazing head of yours?"

She whipped around and pinned him to the seat with her gaze. "Do you really expect me to believe you and Jessica aren't lovers?"

"Yes." He forced himself to keep his arms at his sides instead of taking Vicki by the shoulders and shaking some sense into her. She was the only woman in his life, and had been since he walked into TechTronics. Why was she so distrustful of him? "There is nothing between me and Neimier. The woman's a barracuda, and I've avoided her as much as possible. I like determined women, but not aggressive women like her." He lowered his voice and leaned toward her. "More like the woman you were in the elevator that Friday night."

Her lashes swept down, but not before he observed regret filling her eyes.

"Vicki." He couldn't bear not touching her, so took her hands and waited until her gaze met his. "I didn't lie to you when I said I wasn't involved with anyone, and I'm not going to begin lying now. There is nothing between Ms. Neimier and me. You've got to trust me on this. And trust me, what we have is special, not something to feel guilty about."

Her lower lip quivered. "I want to, Joe, but … "

A fist closed around his heart at the 'but'. He couldn't, *wouldn't*, let her go, not until he was able to free her from the ghostly ex's hold. "Will you answer one question for me?"

Her gaze turned wary even as she answered him. "Of course. I haven't lied to you, either."

"Do you want me?" He thought she craved his touch, but he had to know for certain. Even with her telling him earlier she was willing to have a relationship with him, he needed it confirmed with recent events.

Her gaze lowered once again, concealing her expression from him, and for a moment he had doubts. She took a deep breath, and her breasts swelled, her nipples pebbling against the thin fabric of her blouse. She shifted slightly against the vinyl seat. Hope flared as he waited. He wanted the answer from her lips. "Yes," she whispered.

"Yes, what?" he pressed, even though he had promised himself he wouldn't. He needed to hear her say the words. Her lashes rose, and passion, lust, and still a bit of apprehension filled her gaze. Her hesitation punched him in the gut. He had a lot of work to do.

"Yes, I want you." While her voice was low, the words were clear. "I want to have a relationship."

Joe let out a breath he didn't even realize he'd been holding. "I want you, too. Day and night."

"Don't say that."

"Why not?" He lifted her right hand and kissed the center of her palm, feeling the slight shiver his kiss produced.

"Because I'm not like other women."

"Damn straight." Her eyes widened. "You're more, and I can't wait until we're alone after business hours. Then I can show you how much I want you and revel in the fact you aren't like other women. Don't let another man's opinion of you ruin mine."

Another shiver shook her slender body just as the cab pulled to a stop. Joe glanced up. They were outside her apartment building. "I hate to cut this short, but we'd better get you packed so we can make our flight."

"You want to help me pack?" Her voice was breathless yet yearning.

"Yep." He opened the door, climbed out, and offered his hand. For once, she didn't even hesitate and placed her palm in his, allowing him to help her from the taxi. Joe moved his lips next to her ear. "I want to make sure you pack the black teddy." He turned and paid the driver, then asked him to wait to take them to the airport. Once the driver agreed, he slipped an arm around Vicki's shoulders and started walking.

"Are you always this physical?" she asked.

"Only with you." He found it was true. He wanted, no, *needed* physical contact with her at all times. It would make keeping their relationship impersonal during business hours difficult, but he'd do it. Once they were off the clock, he wasn't going to hold back. "Does it bother you?"

"Sometimes," she said as they made their way up the steps. As he reached for the door, she said, "I need to get my card key out." She opened her purse and extracted what looked like a credit card, then slipped it into the small slot on the wall.

When he'd arrived on Saturday, someone had been leaving the building, so he hadn't noticed it. After a faint hum, then a click, the green light flashed. He pushed open the door. "Nice security feature."

"It was one of the reasons I moved here." She waved at the security guard behind the desk, a different one than from the weekend. Vicki stopped and talked to the guard about feeding her cat, another nice service of renting in the building, before they went to her apartment.

Once there he was surprised again. She had to unlock two deadbolts along with the heavy door lock. After they entered her apartment, Joe shut the door and stared at it. In addition to the two deadbolts, she had three chains. He hadn't noticed on Saturday. Why so much hardware?

"Break-in?" he asked.

"No." She gestured him forward. "I just like to be safe."

From what? Who the hell had scared her so much she had to lock herself away in her own apartment? The ex, more than likely. He needed to know the whole story, because if this man was still a threat to her, he'd make sure she was safe. Forcing back the urge to question her about it, he sauntered into her living room. On Saturday he'd been too busy concentrating on Vicki to notice much of anything else. He blinked several times, staring. Everything was beige. The carpet, the walls, the sofa, even the bookcase had been stained to match. Was she that much of a perfectionist?

"I'll go pack—alone," she said, leaving the room.

He paced around the compact living space. There were no family photographs. He knew her parents were still around, so why no pictures? Stopping at the bookcase, he ran his fingers over the spines. Shakespeare, Plato, *War and Peace*. Sexy and intellectual.

He moved to the next shelf. Ah, these were more like it. Erotic romance books by different authors and publishers. Picking one at random, he opened it and began reading. *Holy shit!* He slammed the book shut and put it back. The passage he'd read had the hero spanking the heroine, and while it gave him ideas, this wasn't what he needed right now. He was hard enough as it was; reading one of those books was better than watching soft porn. If his Vicki liked reading them, they could have some fun.

Feeling something soft twirl around his ankles, he glanced down and saw her gray cat, entwined around his feet. "Hello, Sly." He reached down and stroked the feline's sleek coat. Before he realized what he was doing, he lifted the feline into his arms and began scratching him behind the ears. The cat gave a soft purr. He could swear Sly was giving him permission to pursue Vicki. Needing to be with her, he strode into her bedroom.

Damn, this woman was a study in opposites. While her living room looked bland and monotonous, her bedroom was a different matter. The walls were painted white, and she'd hung several landscape paintings to brighten up the room. A black suitcase sat open on her bed, and beneath it lay a patchwork quilt. For a moment he wondered if her sheets were the plain cotton type or something sexier. Sexy, he decided, and promised himself he'd find out.

His gaze found her by the walk-in closet, her hand hovering over what looked like a sexy black dress. "Perfect."

Vicki swung around, her hand covering her heart. "You

scared me. And I thought I told you to wait in the living room."

"You did." He grinned as he crossed the room to see what she'd already packed. Setting the cat down, he picked up the item lying on top. "Very nice," he murmured, holding the lacy red teddy by the straps.

"I'm glad you approve." She marched over to him, snatched the garment from his fingers, and put it back in the suitcase. The dress followed.

"What else do you have in there?"

"Joe!" She grabbed his hand before he could investigate.

He glanced up at her, noting her flushed cheeks. "When was the last time you had a man in your bedroom?"

"Saturday."

He frowned, and she laughed. "Remember, you followed me in here then as well."

"True. Before then?" Why was he prying? She had mentioned it had been a while since the ex.

She shook her head and placed her hands on her hips. "To set your mind at ease, Mr. Nosy, I've never had a man in this bedroom except you."

"Hmm. Maybe we should christen the place." He took her hand and raised it to his lips, allowing his breath to caress her knuckles.

"What time does our plane leave?" she asked, her voice breathless.

"One."

Her eyes widened. "It's eleven. We've got just enough time for me to finish packing, get to the airport, check in, and clear security."

"So we miss it. We can take the next one." He drew her into his arms with a soft touch, his lips finding her earlobe and nipping at it. "Think about it, Vicki—us together in your bed, naked. My cock pumping into your wet pussy, my lips on your breasts as I bring you closer to your climax. But at the last minute, I stop moving. Then I flip you onto your stomach and take you doggy style, hard and fast until you're screaming." Oh, hell, he was arousing himself with his words.

Her hips pressed against his, and she let out a tiny moan.

"Just say the word, my beautiful Vicki." He cradled her closer. For a moment he figured she was going to give into him, then she leaned back, and he gazed into her eyes. Regret filled them.

"Joe … "

"No, precious." He placed his finger against her lips. "You're right, now is not the time. I want you to trust me. The next move is yours." With those words, he released her and strode out of the room so he wouldn't give into temptation.

Ten minutes later he yelled, "We've got to go."

"I'm coming," she called back.

Her words slammed into his libido and he smiled. Oh yes, he'd have her coming, all right. All night long.

"WANT TO JOIN the mile-high club?" Joe asked, after the pilot announced their cruising altitude and turned off the seat belt sign.

"Joe!" She glanced around. It didn't seem as if anyone was paying attention to them, not that it mattered all that much; outside of the flight attendant and pilots, they were the only people on the charter plane. She hadn't been able to believe it when she and Joe were escorted out onto the tarmac. She'd stared at him as they boarded the small plane, but he'd grinned and said, "Perks."

He'd guided her past the single seat to a pair of double ones. Now she knew why. The man was outrageous, and she didn't have much resistance where he was concerned. Excitement surged through her veins, because with Joe she was able to be herself. She'd almost given in to him at her apartment. She couldn't get the images of them on her red satin sheets, fucking, out of her mind. But they had a plane to catch—of course, at the time, she didn't know it was a private plane.

"What?" A devilish grin curved his lips. "No one will notice." His palm rested against her thigh.

Heat penetrated through the skirt with a direct effect on her pussy. If she hadn't been so aroused already this would have gotten her there, and fast. She shifted in the leather seat. She'd never flown in such luxury before, and while she liked the extra room, they couldn't … "You can't be serious?"

"No?" He raised an eyebrow as his fingers inched up her hem. "With your skirt covering us when you straddle me, who would know?"

"Everyone." With a gentle grip, she removed his questing fingers and put them on his armrest before she turned from his blatant sexual gaze and stared out the window. God, it was hard not to give into the excitement running through her body, but they were in a public place. *But I had sex in an elevator with him.* That was different. Only the two of them knew about it. Warm skin against her jaw brought her out of her thoughts. He applied soft pressure until her gaze met his. She was becoming addicted to his skin against hers.

Joe leaned down and brushed a light kiss against her lips, then raised his head. "You're so easy to tease. I said the next move was yours, and I meant it."

When the words penetrated, she almost smiled. Yes, the next action was hers. Slipping her hand behind his neck, she lowered her lips to his. First she gave him a teasing kiss, but then each kiss became, little by little, longer and deeper. She enjoyed the way their tongues tangled together, dueling with each other. She whimpered when he pulled back and knew she was a goner the second she viewed the fire in his eyes. Satisfaction filled her. He wasn't as unaffected as he appeared.

"Let's go to the bathroom," he said, undoing his seat belt and reaching for hers.

Grasping his fingers, she lifted them from the metal buckle to her cheek. "No, Joe."

He gazed at her, his blue eyes blazing with passion. She'd take care of his passion, but she wasn't going to have sex in an airplane lavatory—or at least, not today.

The flight attendant stopped next to his seat. "Excuse me, can I get you anything right now?"

"Yes." Victoria smiled at the woman, a wicked idea already forming in her mind. "We need a couple of blankets, please."

"Of course." Within minutes the flight attendant handed her two good-sized blankets wrapped in plastic.

"Thank you." Victoria took them and gave them to Joe. The attendant continued, "I'll be dimming the cabin lights in a few minutes so you can rest. I'll have your meal ready in two hours."

"Thank you," Victoria said with a smile.

"What are you up to?" he asked after the flight attendant walked away.

With a grin, she undid her seat belt, kissed his cheek, and stood. "I'll be right back." She slid by him and down the aisle.

Inside the luxurious lavatory, she stared at herself in the mirror. Who was this woman? Her cheeks glowed with excitement, her eyes danced with mischief, and her body tingled with sexual need. Never had a man made her crave his caresses, his kisses, or his cock the way Joe did. It frightened her, but at the same time desire flowed through her. Her cheeks flushed, and she knew it was from arousal rather than embarrassment.

"What do you want?" Joe. A simple answer. She wanted him. But was she ready to take the risk on a relationship? She took a deep breath, because there was always going to be a risk to her heart no matter what.

The answer came back in an instant. Yes! Time to start living again. She'd never had this sexual connection with Derek, and they'd been engaged. Heck, sex with Derek hadn't gotten beyond the kindling stage, but with Joe it was a raging forest fire that continued to build. She needed to see where this relationship could go, to grasp the need with both hands and see where it led her. It was time to allow Vicki out and let her have control. A little laugh escaped her lips. She wasn't schizophrenic. She was very aware she kept a part of herself under tight control. The wild kinky side. While a part of her still worried she could be risking her job, she also trusted Joe when he said that wasn't an issue.

True, she didn't work for him, and she didn't report to him for anything. They were peers, not one a subordinate to the other. Plus, after watching him for the last six months, she'd never noticed him make a pass at anyone regardless of the rumors circulating about him. He'd been telling the truth about Jessica Neimier. Her heart lightened.

Time for her to take control. Joe had been calling the shots since their encounter in the elevator. Now, as he'd said, it was her turn. Power filled her veins.

Being cocooned in their seats gave her some measure of safety and was a lot less obvious than the two of them walking into one of the bathrooms together. There wouldn't be much room in the seats. All the more fun. She'd never thought about having her movements restricted in some way before. Oh, she'd read about it, but now she was excited thinking how those limitations would heighten their pleasure.

She took a deep breath, lifted her skirt and slid her panties off. Today she was wearing thigh-high stockings without a garter belt to make her feel beautiful and sexy. She folded her underwear into a small bundle and concealed it in her hand. Forcing air into her lungs, she opened the door and walked back to her seat, heart pounding.

Joe gave her an inquiring look when she returned. She just smiled, feeling wicked, scooted by him and tucked her underwear into her purse. Before she sat down she spread the blanket on the seat, then as she sat down, she lifted the back of her skirt. She'd rather get the blanket wet than her clothing. Goose bumps danced along her skin when her bare butt connected with the cool soft fabric. "Vicki?"

"Yes." She lowered the shade on the window as the cabin lights dimmed and they heard the announcement of the start of the in-flight movie. Good, at least the cabin would be semi-dark. She took the other blanket from his lap, arranged it over herself, covering from just below her breasts almost to her knees.

"What are you up to?" His voice dropped to a husky, sexy tone, sending shivers of awareness through her bloodstream; his eyes were blazing.

"Me?" She worked her skirt up beneath the blanket and tucked the fabric into the waistband—this way, there was nothing in his way.

"Yes, you." Joe stared at her with amusement.

Without answering, she grasped his left hand and brought it under the blanket. He inhaled deeply when she parted her legs, allowing his fingers to rest on her naked pussy.

"Fuck," he whispered before glancing around. She bit back a giggle. They were alone.

"I'm making the first move, Joe. Now it's your turn."

Reaching up, he flipped off the small light, making their area darker. Then he pressed a button and the armrest between them slid down between the seats. "Lean back," he ordered. While he hadn't planned on this, her bold move made his blood boil. The nice thing about a charter flight was privacy. Vicki pushed the button, and her seat not only slid back, it reclined, raising her legs and opening her up to him.

His gaze clashed with hers and he withdrew his hand from beneath the blanket, twisting in his seat, his right hand diving beneath the blanket. This time there was no hesitation. His fingers parted her pussy lips and he thrust one digit deep into her welcoming depths.

He stifled her moan of pleasure with a hard, deep kiss, his tongue acting out what he planned to do with his fingers. Never breaking the kiss, he stroked her with one finger, then two, then three, caressing her harder and faster as her body became more aroused.

She was so wet. He would never get enough of her. When she opened her legs wider, allowing him greater penetration, he knew this woman was the right one for him—bold and adventurous. She was giving him the gift of her trust, and he wouldn't abuse it. Her body began to tremble, and she tightened around his fingers. Yes, she was getting close.

He thrust into her harder and quicker, his thumb on her clit. Her moans were suppressed by his kisses as they grew more and more demanding. She met him kiss for kiss. Her hips arched up. She was about to climax. He thrust his fingers deep into her, and he flicked his thumb over her clit as she exploded around him, her cry of release smothered by his mouth.

He let her orgasm subside before removing all but one finger. With a gentle caress, he started all over again. He wanted her to get her pleasure and then some; she was trusting him and he was going to make sure she enjoyed herself.

She tore her lips from his, drawing in big gasps of breath. "Joe?" Her eyes were clouded with passion, but there was also a question in them.

"You're so moist, so hot." He whispered in her ear as his lips caressed the lobe, and he was glad she'd left her hair up. His tongue laved the delicate shell as he continued to tease her. Her breathing increased when he slipped a second finger into her wetness. "Tight, warm, and welcoming, just like I remembered." He kissed her neck before moving back to her ear and nipping the lobe. "Do you know how hard it was for me on Saturday to play the gentleman and not try to seduce you into bed?"

"It wouldn't have taken much."

Joe groaned. She was finally opening up to him. Pleasure shot through his veins. "Now she tells me," he whispered, and she let out a little laugh. "Feel my fingers, sweetheart, knowing I'd rather be thrusting my cock into you hard and fast." He moved them in short bursts as his thumb played with her clit.

"Oh, God, Joe." Her words were breathless as she arched her pelvis toward his thrusting fingers. Her climax was building.

"Again, baby. Come for me. Let me feel your pleasure, knowing later tonight we'll be together in a big bed, naked and fucking." Her sex tightened around his fingers as if it was trying to pull them in. "That's it," he crooned, as she pressed down hard against his hand. "Tonight I'm going to pleasure you so much, you'll scream. We'll come together so many times. I'll use my mouth, my fingers, and my cock all over your body."

He captured her lips just as her second climax ripped through her. He stilled his fingers, but his thumb kept moving over her clit as wave after wave roared through her body. Her hips bucked against his hand. He let her do what she wanted. This was all for her.

When he released her mouth, her head fell limp against the seat, her breathing harsh. He contemplated dropping to his knees in the small space and sucking her to another wild climax, but decided that particular pleasure could wait until tonight. More than ever he wanted to hear her scream out her orgasm.

With care, he pulled his fingers from her sex then brought them to his lips, tasting her precious nectar. He watched her for several minutes before asking, "Okay?"

Her expression was pretended dread. "I don't think I can breathe."

He chuckled.

"Wicked man, making me come a second time." Her lashes rose, revealing green eyes alight with passion and satisfaction. Gone was the prim and proper Victoria and in her place sat wild, wanton Vicki. He grinned; he had finally gotten her to release her wild side.

Wetness seeped from between her thighs. She glanced over at Joe. His cock strained against the fabric of his pants. Her teeth tugged at her lower lip. She wanted him to feel pleasure too. She pressed the button, and the seat moved upright. She straightened the front of her skirt until it covered her once again. Then she took the blanket from her lap and folded it, acting as if nothing had happened. Turning toward Joe, she placed the blanket over his legs and slipped her left hand beneath. Her palm caressed his fabric-covered hardness.

"Vicki." His voice was gruff as he curled his fingers around her wrist.

"Your turn," she whispered, prying away his fingers. "My experience with you in the elevator showed me just how virile you are." She adjusted the blanket covering his lap, making sure it covered his groin and his legs cradled most of the fabric. "I would suggest you keep your legs together so we don't lose the blanket." His climax wouldn't be as easy to contain as hers.

Joe sucked in a deep breath when she undid the snap and lowered the zipper on his slacks, freeing his cock. Oh, Lord, his right hand gripped the armrest like a lifeline as her fingers caressed his dick.

"Naughty man," she whispered, her breath brushing his cheek. "Leaving home without briefs. I never took you as a man who would go commando in public."

"I like the freedom." He struggled to get the words out.

"So do I."

Her words only increased his hardness. As her fingers curved around his cock, he could barely control himself from thrusting into her palm. "Vicki." He said her name with a groan as she gave him a long stroke. Never had a woman's hands felt so good. His adventurous, spirited Vicki.

"Yes, Joe." Her breath skimmed his ear. "I'm going to jack you off, here and now."

Did he want to stop her? Hell, no. This was Vicki, the sexually explosive woman he craved. "Condom," he whispered; thank goodness the flight attendant was in the galley at the front of plane and they were in the back.

"What?" Her eyes were blazing with desire and lust.

"There's a condom in my pocket. Take it out and put it on, so I won't spread my come all over this damn plane." While the blanket would take the brunt of his desire, he'd rather not worry about too much of a mess.

A grin teased her lips as she found the small packet. She opened it and placed the condom over the tip of his cock, holding it in place.

"What have you done?" he asked when her warm fingers encircled his dick, skin to skin.

"Don't worry." She shifted herself in her seat, sliding even closer to him. "I'm holding the end of the condom over the tip. You'll come into it. I need to feel you and only you, not some damn rubber."

"God, baby." He arched his hips as she teased him with her gentle touch, moving up and down his cock. Once in a while she'd caress the head with the pad of her thumb, careful not to snag the condom, her breathing rapid against his face.

She never increased her pace, but it didn't matter. He was ready to explode anyway. She began squeezing right below the head of his cock. *Shit!* Joe clamped his lips together to stop himself from shouting out. The tingles began at the base of his spine, and his balls tightened.

His body stiffened, and he grasped the back of her head, bringing her mouth to his as he erupted. Vicki kept stroking him as he emptied himself into the latex. He sagged back against the seat, eyes closed.

She kissed his cheek. "Ah, Joe. What do we do about the condom?"

Forcing his eyes open, he slipped a hand beneath the blanket. He slid his fingers past the head of his dick to grasp the condom between thumb and forefinger. "I've got it." His cock jumped as she brushed her fingers over the head and she removed her hand. Carefully, he slipped the condom off. "Tuck me back into my pants and zip me up," he whispered. This was pure torture, he decided seconds later as her touch shot straight through him. By the time she had him neatly back into his pants and zipped, he was hard again. "Open the airsickness bag." She did as he asked. He took it from her and deposited the condom in it, then stood. "I'll be right back." Joe made his way to the lavatory. Once inside, he disposed of the condom, then undid his pants and let them drop. He threw back his head, breathing through his nose. His body still hummed with need as he fisted his dick. After several minutes of self-pleasure, he cleaned up and made his way back to her.

Vicki's seat was in a reclined position once again and her eyes were closed. The blankets were folded at her feet. Joe noticed a new air sickness bag sitting on his seat. He lifted it before resuming his place. There was something in it. Opening the bag, he peeked in.

He let out a groan and turned his head to see her watching him, her eyes twinkling with excitement.

"Just something for you to think about," she whispered, before closing her eyes once again.

Joe bit back a growl of frustration. This woman was going to be the death of him, but he didn't care. Folding the paper bag and its contents with consideration, he slipped it into his carry-on.

His dick had grown hard once again, but what could he expect when she'd just let him know she was still naked beneath her skirt? The little tease had given him her panties.

VICTORIA SMILED AS she walked off the plane in New Orleans, *sans* panties. She didn't know how she'd had the nerve not only to climax on their flight from his fingers, but also for her to do the same to him. Something inside her had taken over. *Vicki.*

She sounded schizophrenic, but she wasn't. She knew damn well she'd been suppressing her sexual side for years. All it took was Joe to make her free. A weight had been lifted from her.

Of course, a year of celibacy hadn't been a good idea, either. If they hadn't been trapped in the elevator she might have been able to suppress Vicki for a lot longer, but no more. Vicki didn't like being prim and proper. And if she was honest with herself, she didn't either.

Her fingers curled around the handles of the plastic bag she was holding. Joe had run into one of the gift shops, bought something, and returned. He made her promise not to peak. She watched as Joe retrieved their luggage, and she enjoyed the way his muscles played beneath his shirt. She'd like it even more tonight, when her fingers caressed those same muscles as he fucked her. She shivered in delight.

The second they stepped outside the airport, hot sticky air

found its way beneath her clothing, causing instant moisture to cling to her body. She glanced around for the taxi stand. Her heart stopped as she spotted a familiar figure a short distance away. *Derek?* It couldn't be.

Blinking, her vision cleared, and the man wasn't there. Shaking her head, she banished all thoughts of him. Obviously she was still reacting to the email from this morning. Derek couldn't be in New Orleans. It was impossible. He couldn't know where she was.

She turned back to Joe, who had his hand raised, beckoning to a limousine as it pulled to the curb. A uniformed driver climbed out. "Mr. Bradshaw, Ms. Collins, welcome to New Orleans. I'll take care of the luggage. Please be seated inside, out of this heat."

Vicki glanced over at Joe, who was grinning at her. He took the plastic bag from her, opened the door and leaned inside. His eyes twinkled with mischief when he straightened.

"Lift your skirt and sit with your bare ass on the seat," he whispered as she started to climb in.

Her heart sped up, and she couldn't resist glancing at him over her shoulder. But Joe had moved, blocking anyone's view of her. Stepping into the limo, she saw a small towel placed on the leather seat she lifted her skirt and sank down onto the soft fabric. Her pussy gushed at what Joe might be planning.

"I thought this might be better than a sizzling, oppressive cab ride to the hotel," Joe said, sliding in next to her, his thigh against hers.

"It was very thoughtful of you," she said, before turning to gaze out the window. But she didn't see anything, her thoughts filled with Joe.

"You'll find I'm very thoughtful." He leaned forward and raised the privacy panel between them and the driver.

Vicki swallowed. Her heart stopped. What was he planning

now? "What are you up to, Joe?"

"Oh, I'm up all right."

She couldn't help herself. She giggled at his words and glanced at his crotch. As the car began moving, Joe opened the minibar, pulled out a glass of ice, and set it on the floor.

"Lift your skirt to your waist and open those gorgeous legs for me. I want to have some fun with my pussy."

"Your pussy?" She exposed herself to his gaze. Oh, Lord, she was so wet she was dripping onto the seat. Wickedness flowed through her.

"Yes, mine." Joe slid to his knees, pushing her thighs apart with his body. He pulled her ass to the edge of the seat, keeping the towel under her. "Hook your legs over my shoulders."

"Joe," she started to protest, not sure if she was ready for this step.

"Do it," he ordered, and Vicki found herself obeying him. Okay, maybe she was ready. His dominant, stern voice turned her on.

Tingles of excitement ran straight to her pussy. Ice clinked in the glass, and then Joe's fingers were at her entrance. "Oh, dear God," she moaned, arching as he placed his tongue into her hot core. He had an ice cube in his mouth, creating a delicious mixture of coolness with her heat. The ice mixed with her body heat and melting water slid down her folds as Joe licked her, slowly, tortuously. After one cube melted, ice jangled as he fished around the glass for another piece.

Oh, shit. She was already on edge. Pleasure swept up her spine, making her shiver. She didn't know how long she could take this. So good, yet so wicked. As scandalous as they were on the plane? They were alone then; the flight attendant was in the front of the plane and they'd been in the back. Here, they were in the back of a limo being driven to their hotel, and Lord only knew what the driver was thinking. Even with the security partition up he could guess at what they were doing. All rational thought fled as Joe inserted an ice cube into her pussy and began sucking. Unable to help herself, Vicki pushed herself into his mouth. Her belly tightened and her orgasm was seconds away. The tinkling of ice reached her ears. This time he placed it on her clit.

Vicki bit her lip to prevent herself from screaming as she climaxed, and climaxed hard. She thrashed against the seat, her legs tightening around Joe as he continued to suck her and play with her clit.

She collapsed against the seat, exhausted, and Joe raised his head, grinning at her. He licked her juices from his lips. "Didn't I say I was thoughtful? I figured you might need cooling off." He lowered her legs from his shoulders.

"I think you're the one who needs cooling off." She sat up and cupped his hard cock through his pants.

"Later." Leaning over, he captured her lips with his. Seconds later, the car stopped. "We're here," Joe said. "Lift your ass up."

After she obeyed, Joe slid her skirt down and pulled the towel from underneath her. He folded the fabric and put it back into the plastic bag. He adjusted his cock and returned to his seat. When they emerged from the limo, Vicki wasn't sure if the driver was smiling because it was his job to do so or because he knew what they'd been doing. And did she care? A thrill of naughtiness swept through her veins.

She forced herself not to squirm at her nakedness beneath her skirt. This was becoming a habit, running around without her panties. A sexy habit. She fought back a giggle at her silly thoughts.

A bellman jogged up to them, took their luggage, and led them into the hotel. People were milling all over the elegant lobby area. Joe took her hand and guided her to the registration desk. Within ten minutes, not only were they on their way up to the hotel room, but they were also checked into the conference. Vicki scanned the list of activities as they walked down the hall.

Joe opened the door with a flourish, and she sauntered inside to a large sitting area with a sofa and chair. Giving the place a quick glance, she observed two doors. Behind her, Joe was talking with the bellman as she walked over to the window and looked out. The Big Easy. She could see the French Quarter from their room, and it was just coming to life as the sun faded. Her heart hurt for the Crescent City.

A hurricane had devastated the area several years ago, but it was recovering, albeit slowly. The city was fighting back and would be better than ever. If there was one thing she'd learned over the years, people were resilient. Like she was after her grandmother had died.

She turned from the view. Joe stood by one of the doors. Tiptoeing over, she peeked inside the room.

An extra large king-size bed dominated the space, and their luggage was placed on the rack at the end of the bed. Without saying a word, she checked out the second room. This one was smaller and held a more modest queen-size bed. While she knew they were going to be sleeping together, at least the suite gave the pretense they were in separate beds.

Was she jumping the gun in thinking that using the second room was not in the plan? She shook her head. Joe had whispered such delicious naughty things to her, and she no longer possessed the will to resist him. A fling, a fantasy come to life, that's all she needed to remember. Within days it would be over and they'd return to reality. Or would they? Before she could dwell on the question, Joe pulled her into his arms.

"You're wearing too many clothes." His breath brushed her ear.

"I believe we have a reception to attend." She extricated

herself from his embrace before she could give in to the temptation to sink into him. They were here on business, and she needed to remember that.

"Victoria is back." The regret in his voice came through loud and clear.

"Don't say that." She whirled around, hands on hips. She hated it when he commented on her proper side. She was one person and one of them had to be sensible.

"It's true." He folded his arms over his chest as he watched her.

"I *am* Victoria." She gritted her teeth after she said the words.

Joe shook his head, his eyes alight with impishness. "Victoria is the prim, proper persona you put on. Vicki is the real you. When you choose to let her out, that is."

She wanted to argue with him, but knew she couldn't. He was right, damn it. "I'm both Victoria and Vicki—she's the same person. So quit thinking I'm two people."

"Ah, but you are." He took her hand and raised it to his lips. "You have a public side and a private side. Victoria is the public side, whereas Vicki is the private side. Every once in a while, the private side slips out."

"At inappropriate moments."

Joe frowned. "Is what we did on the plane bothering you? What I did in the car?"

She shook her head. She wasn't bothered by what happened, but ... "I'm just having a hard time believing I was so uninhibited." Even though she had enjoyed every second of it, her mind was still playing catch-up. Yes, she wanted Joe. But a part of her psyche kept warning her this might be a disaster.

"What?" He cupped her chin in his palm. "You're so beautiful when you come. Whether it's from my fingers, my mouth, or my cock. You make me wild."

Heat rose to her cheeks. His words were explicit. Would she ever get used to it? Probably not, but it still excited her. "But making you … " Her words trailed off.

"Come." He rested his forehead against hers. "There's absolutely nothing wrong with anything we've done together. We're consenting adults. Trust me, if I'd have thought for one second we'd have been caught, I wouldn't have allowed it to happen."

His words rang true in her heart. "I believe you, but … "

"Don't be embarrassed. I love the way you come apart from my touch. And your touch does the same thing to me. I've never had it happen to me before." His voice was husky.

"Really?" A tingle of empowerment filled her body.

"Really." He gazed down at her. "I've never let a woman touch me in public, nor taken her in public as I have with you. I have no control where you're concerned."

His words thrilled her, because she had so little control around him as well. "Thank you." Maybe they weren't so different after all. She captured the thought and pulled it around her like a blanket.

"You're welcome. Let's check out the bed." He tightened his grip on her.

She laughed as she spun out of his arms. "Not yet, Mr. Bradshaw. We've got a reception to attend, then we'll test the mattress." She sashayed into the main bedroom, picked up her bag, then walked out. She gave him a shy glance over her shoulder while she made her way to the smaller bedroom. "And maybe test a few other things in this suite." She disappeared, and a click sounded as the bathroom door closed.

Joe laughed before going into the main bedroom. The little witch was teasing him again, but then he could tease her all night long while they were at the reception. Oh, he'd be careful he didn't cross the line in public, but he knew they'd be dancing, and he could tease the hell out of her as they moved together. By the time they got back to their room, she'd be so hot and ready. And he'd take her in more ways than one tonight. He still had a few surprises in store.

Chapter Seven

oe's breath whooshed out in a hiss when Vicki emerged from the bathroom. "Dear Lord," he whispered.

"You like?" She twirled around.

"Like?" He struggled to get the words past the restriction crowding his throat. The black dress molded to her perfect breasts, and her nipples were erect against the fabric. It gathered at her waist, showing off just how slender she was, and the skirt … what there was of it showed off her long legs. He swallowed. "I'm never going to survive the reception."

A husky laugh escaped her lips, and Joe liked this side of her, playful and seductive. There were times her rigid side was appropriate, but he liked it far better when she buried that part of her.

"You'd better survive." She crossed the room, raised her hands, and fixed his tie. "I have plans for us tonight."

He couldn't help himself. He raised his hand and tweaked her very erect nipples. "So do I," he said, sliding his palms around to her back and down over her butt, enjoying the silky feel of the dress against his skin. He moved his hands lower until he came to the hem of the dress. "What are you wearing underneath?"

"Not much."

Her soft-spoken words went straight to his groin, and he sprang erect. Inch by inch, he tunneled his fingers beneath the fabric, encountering her stocking and garters, then bare skin. "Please don't tell me you're going in the raw." He'd go insane if she was, and there was no way he was letting her out of this room without panties of some sort.

"Okay, I won't." She smoothed her palms over his shoulders.

He groaned as he tightened his fingers around the silky globes of her ass. "I need to fuck you."

She gave another husky laugh as she smoothed her palms over the front of his jacket and further down until she cupped his hard cock and gave it a squeeze. "Later." She shifted and widened her stance. "But I can assure you I'm not naked." The tiny scrap of material rubbed against his fingertips. Their gazes locked. "I'm wearing a thong," she confirmed.

He traced the material between her butt cheeks, his fingers curving around to feel the heat from her barely-covered sex. Slipping a finger beneath the thong, he teased her already swollen clit. "Later I'm going to enjoy tearing this scrap of fabric from your body." He removed his finger, sliding it into his mouth before stepping away from her luscious body. Before he forgot he was a civilized man. Before he started falling for her.

She walked her fingers up his erection and on up to his chest as she licked her lips. "I'm looking forward to it."

WHILE JOE HAD never considered himself the jealous type, he resented every man in the room when they walked in. They were all staring at his woman. *His woman.* Funny how those words fit so perfectly.

He had never thought about claiming a woman as his until Vicki. She might think he wanted her for sex, but there was more.

He enjoyed her company, her sense of humor, and yes, the explosive sex. Tonight he'd see just how adventurous she was.

Joe introduced Vicki to several people before pulling her out onto the makeshift dance floor. He spun her into his arms, cradling her close to him, his palm against her spine. "You've got every man in this room lusting after you." He spoke softly, close to her ear.

"The women aren't immune to you, either," she said, her tone light but wary.

His palms slid to settle at the small of her back, his fingers playing over her hips, pressing her tight against him as they moved around the dance floor. "You're the only woman I care about." Joe realized it was true.

"That's a nice thing to say." There was disbelief in her tone.

"I mean it." He maneuvered them off the dance floor. "I want to show you something." He took her hand as he led her through a doorway, then past another door marked "private." He pushed open the French doors, and they were out on a balcony.

A sultry breeze ruffled his hair and slid over his skin. He needed a private spot with her where no one would interrupt them, even if it were only for a few precious minutes. Gathering her close, he trapped her against the wall before capturing her lips.

Their tongues collided and dueled before retreating and tangling once again. Their kisses were hot, moist, and frantic. He couldn't get enough of her.

And she must feel the same about him. Her hands were all over him, his shoulders, his back, down to his ass. Squeezing his butt.

He pushed his knee between her legs, nudging them apart as he skimmed his fingers down her sides, burrowing underneath her short skirt to cup her sex.

"Joe," she protested.

"No one can see us." A small stone balcony wall protected

their lower bodies. If anyone happened to look, they'd think he was enjoying her kisses.

Her thong was soaked. Pushing aside the fabric, his fingers delved into her moistness. She tightened around him as their lips met once again. Joe stroked her, delighted in the way she kept thrusting against his hand and her hot, uncontrollable kisses. Soon her body convulsed with her release. He grinned against her lips, pleased he could make her come so fast.

She tore her mouth away from his, drawing in deep breaths before she rested her forehead against his shoulder.

"You're so beautiful when you come," he whispered, wiggling his fingers still deep within her.

"Joe." She whispered his name like a plea; a shudder shook her body as she clung to him.

"You're so damn responsive. All I can think about is fucking you. I don't care where we are." His lips brushed across her cheek. "You laid out on the floor, against the wall while I impale you on my cock. Outside in the burning New Orleans sun riding in one of the horse-drawn carriages as I use my fingers on you." Her fingers tightened on his ass, pulling him closer. "In the shower with me directing water against your clit, making you come harder. On the kitchen table, with you spread out on your stomach as I fuck you from behind. Tied up on my bed, begging for my touch as I tease you with a feather."

He sucked in a breath when her lips touched his neck, and then she licked his skin. "I want those things too," she whispered. "I want all of them. I want to be your love slave."

If he was hard before, now he was like steel. He nuzzled her hair while she teased his skin with kisses and licks. They couldn't walk out of the party after only being there an hour, but he was tempted.

Flexing his fingers inside her, she tightened around the digits as she thrust her hips forward. "Just think, tonight I'm going to take you back to our room." He worked her hair out of the way until his lips were right next to her ear. "First I'll strip this dress off, and since you're not wearing a bra, I'll draw your nipples deep into my mouth, sucking them until they become taut and almost painful."

She slid her palms down his back, her nails scraping against the fabric of his jacket, and she let out a moan.

"Then I'll unhook your garter belt and roll the nylons down your legs. I'll rip the thong from your body before lifting you onto the mattress." Joe drew in a deep breath when she slipped her hands down to his butt and her fingers clenched his ass, and then moved back up to his waist. She didn't say anything, but he heard her panting.

"Once you're in bed, I'll tie your wrists to the headboard, then I'll spread your legs and tie them as well. You'll be open wide. Very wide. I'll place pillows under you so your pussy is raised to me. Then I'll kneel on the mattress and lower my mouth to your sweet sex. I'll lick, nip, and suck, tasting your succulent essence until it flows all over my mouth." While he spoke, she undid his belt and zipper, letting his pants slip down his legs. She slipped her fingers over the head of his pulsing cock. Joe fought against a groan as she teased him with a look of pure bliss on her face. With her caressing him, he feared he wouldn't be able to contain himself. Maybe he should've worn underwear.

"Once you've climaxed from my lips," he continued, "I'll add my fingers to the mix. My tongue will make love to you while I stroke your clit, bringing you to another orgasm, and before it can subside, I'll rise over you, kissing you, letting you taste yourself on my lips, before I plunge into your hot wetness, filling you on the first thrust."

"Oh, yes!" Her second climax of the night came then. Her

body bucked, his fingers buried deep inside her while her grip tightened around his cock.

God, she was so beautiful. Satisfaction he was able to make her climax curled in his belly as he waited until her body calmed down before speaking. "You think you're spent after I've made you come five times, but we're only getting started."

Her eyes flashed in surprise. "Oh, God, Joe. Fuck me. Here. Now. I need you in me."

Her words were like an aphrodisiac. "I thought we were going to wait until we had a bed."

She lifted her head, her green eyes blazing with need and lust. "Now!" He was powerless to resist her. Letting his fingers slide out of her warmth, he guided her hands away from his cock. He slid his finger beneath the fabric of the thong, slid it down her long legs. "Hold on to my shoulders," he whispered. She did as he said, while he lifted one foot at a time to remove the thong. As he stood, he slipped it into his jacket pocket before he pulled out a condom. He pressed it into her palm and lifted her into his arms.

"Slip it on." He gritted his teeth when she smoothed the latex down his shaft. "Now." He lifted her at the waist. "Legs around me and guide me into you." He endured her all encompassing touch as she placed him at her opening. The second her hand left him, he thrust.

"Ah," she breathed, burying her face against his neck and clutching his shoulders.

"You're so tight. So hot. I love the way you grip my cock inside you." He was barely holding on to his control.

"And you're so hard. You feel like steel pushing into me, hard and demanding."

Joe pulled back and shoved forward. At least there was a wall behind her back, or he was sure they would've tumbled over from the force of his thrusts.

"That's it, Joe," she whispered. "Fuck me. Give it to me. I want you."

Her words inflamed him even more, and his control snapped. This wasn't going to be a gentle fuck. He was out of control. He began to pound at will, all the time knowing it would never be enough. He covered her mouth, smothering her cries of ecstasy as she climaxed around him. He trust into her two more times before his balls tensed, and he let go of his own orgasm. Vicki's legs tightened around his waist as Joe braced his arms against the wall, drawing in deep, labored breaths. She was still pulsing around him, as though trying to suck him deeper inside.

Loud voices and laughter from below jolted him back to reality. Smothering a curse, he lifted her off his cock, setting her on her feet. "Okay?" he asked when she wobbled.

"Oh, yeah." Her green eyes were languid, her hair tousled, her lips swollen from his kisses.

Using his handkerchief, Joe wiped her pussy, then removed the condom and attended to himself. It wasn't easy to stuff his fast hardening cock into his pants, but he did it. Then he helped Vicki back into her thong and straightened her clothing. "Your hair's mussed and you've got no lipstick."

She leaned against the wall. "I can't believe … yes, I can. Why do I have no control where you're concerned?" Her gaze, so slumberous just seconds ago, was now filled with questions.

"Maybe because I don't, either." He wasn't going to ask why or how. All he knew was that they belonged together. It was more than sex. No woman could take his control away the way she could, but it was more. It was her humor, her work ethic, hell, everything about her that drew him in. He bent and retrieved her small evening purse from where it had fallen onto the cement. He pressed it into her palm. "Do you think you can walk to the ladies' room?"

She closed her eyes, then inhaled deeply before her lashes lifted. "Yes." She moved toward the French doors, but stopped when she realized he was right beside her. "I'll go alone."

His first instinct was to protest, but then he realized how it might look if he accompanied her. Her hair was rumpled more than enough for people to speculate about what she'd been doing. There was no sense in confirming it. "Meet you at the bar in five minutes."

Seconds later, she glided through the door and out of his sight. Joe retreated to the railing and inhaled the sultry New Orleans air, hoping he could keep his hands off her when she returned.

VICTORIA STARED AT herself in the mirror. She was glowing, there was no other word to describe it. Her cheeks were flushed, her eyes bright, her hair in disarray, and her lips puffy. Shaking her head, she found a small comb in her bag and pulled it through her hair, trying to restore some order to it.

Fine tremors still tingled between her legs, reminding her of what she and Joe had just done out on the balcony. A shiver of excitement shot through her body at the thought of doing it again in the privacy of their suite.

And what had she said? She wanted to be his love slave. All because he talked about tying her up. A thrill of anticipation ran up her spine. She closed her eyes and forced air into her lungs. He was fulfilling each one of her fantasies as if he'd read her most secret desires. A smile crept along her lips. She wanted him to fulfill all her secret desires. She trusted him. Joe wasn't like Derek.

Thinking his name was like a cold shower. No, Derek was in the past. Joe was the present. He wouldn't hurt her like Derek had. Joe made her feel so cherished, so important, as if she were the only woman for him, and he never put her down for her desires.

Concentrate on how Joe makes you feel. After a few minutes, she was calmer and able to push Derek back to the dark recesses of her mind where he belonged.

After restoring her hair, she put on new lipstick and left the bathroom. She turned her head sharply when a shadow caught her gaze. Nothing there. *Relax and enjoy.* She found Joe lounging in the bar area. With a smile, she laid a hand on his shoulder.

"Hi, sweetheart." He faced her before extracting himself from the conversation he'd been engaged in.

"Hi." Desire hit her. She no longer cared what other people thought. She ran the tips of her fingers over his forehead. "I want to be alone with you," she whispered.

Joe hesitated, and she was afraid she'd made a mistake, but then he curved his arm around her waist and stood. "Excuse us," he said, before guiding her out of the room and straight into an empty elevator. He punched the number for their floor before he looked at her. "Ditching the conference?" he asked.

Fear curled in her stomach. Was he angry with her? "I … I couldn't stand being apart from you another second." She bowed her head, staring at the floor. How could she have gotten things so wrong? Did he no longer want her? Did she embarrass him?

His warm palm cupped her chin, urging her face up. "I can't stand being apart from you, either."

His words chased her worries away, and their mouths fused together in a hot, wet kiss. The elevator stopped, and a woman's gasp brought them up for air. Vicki's face grew warm, and she burrowed into Joe's jacket.

"Good evening," said Joe to the couple, pulling Vicki close to him. When the elevator stopped on their floor, he escorted her out of it, down the hall to their room and inside.

"Oh, God, what did she think?" What had happened to her resolution not to care what other people thought?

"Who cares?" Joe rubbed her back. "I think she was jealous as hell of you."

"Of me?" She lifted her head. "Yeah, right."

"Yes, you." He put her at arm's length. "When I look at you, I see a beautiful woman. One who is intelligent, sexy, and downright erotic. Your body has curves in all the right places, your breasts fit into my palms perfectly, your nipples were made for my mouth, and your pussy is where my cock calls home."

Victoria closed her eyes and bit her lower lip, not daring to believe what Joe saw. She knew her flaws and faults—Derek had gone on *ad nauseam* about them. She shivered. How her tits were too tiny, how she was always dry when he wanted to have sex with her. Her stomach cramped.

"I love the way your skin feels against mine, soft to my calluses. The meowing sound you make when I suck your breasts, the way I have to kiss you so no one hears you scream when you climax, your utmost abandonment to pleasure."

"Joe." Her voice was soft, but his words were having an effect on her. Not only was he making her aroused, he was making her believe she was the incredible woman he saw.

Running his palms over her shoulders and down her arms, he brushed her breasts, watching them swell and her nipples pucker. "You're the woman I want more than I want to breathe."

"Shut up and kiss me," she ordered.

His eyes danced with mischief. "My pleasure."

His lips covered hers in a hard, long kiss, and she protested when he ended it. "More," she whispered, trying to pull him back.

"Not yet. I have plans for us, and they don't include making love on the living room floor." Hand in hand, he led her into the bedroom.

The small lamp created a soft glow. When she let out a gasp, he knew she'd seen his handiwork from before they'd attended the party. He'd stripped the comforter and blankets off the bed, fitted the restraints underneath the mattress, and lined up his toys on the nightstand.

"Remember what I said on the balcony?" he whispered, wrapping his arms around her waist and bringing her back against him.

"Yes." The word left her lips in a breathless rush.

"Any objections?" He wasn't going to force her. Talking about it was one thing, doing it was another. She shivered and turned toward him. He glimpsed uncertainty there, but also excitement. His heart leapt. "Trust me?"

She nodded. "Yes, I trust you."

Until this moment, he hadn't realized how much her trust meant to him. Warmth spread from his heart, filling him with exhilaration. "I want to give you so much pleasure. The type of pleasure you deserve as my woman."

"Wh ... when do we start?"

Joe captured her lips once again before he held her at arm's length. *Slow and easy.* "First, I'm going to strip that scrap of a dress from you."

Vicki's breath caught in her throat as Joe's fingers skimmed down to the hem, then he fisted the fabric and pulled it up and off. Cool air caressed her while she stood there in a thong, stockings, and high heels. Part of her wondered if she was as depraved as Derek had once called her. *No.* She shook her head. Joe enjoyed this side of her. He wanted her this way, and she was grateful he did.

"Baby?" Joe cupped her face. "If you don't want to do this, tell me." Concern was etched on his face.

For a moment, she didn't understand what he meant. Oh, hell, she'd shaken her head no, and Joe was reacting. She wet her lips and watched his eyes widen, passion flaring in their depths. "I want this, Joe. I want you."

His breath fanned her face when he exhaled. "I want you, too.

Let's get those shoes off." He kissed her briefly before he knelt. Bracing one hand on his shoulder, she lifted her right foot, then her left. He smiled up at her. "On the bed, my sweet."

She grinned at the endearment; it made her feel special. Her pussy dripped with moisture. She climbed onto the mattress and lay on her back. Feelings of decadence and excitement filled her, along with a little apprehension. She trusted Joe, but things could happen in the heat of passion, bad things. Derek was proof of that.

Feeling his touch against her forehead, she looked up. A tender smile crossed his lips. "Before we start, I want you to have a safe word." He glanced around the room. "Window is your safe word."

"Window," she repeated before leaning up and kissing his stubbled jaw.

"If you become frightened or don't like what I'm doing to you, just say 'window' and I'll stop."

His tone was somber and she wanted to get rid of it. She continued to kiss his jaw, then his neck.

"Vicki, I'm being serious here."

She smiled against his neck before raising her head, meeting his gaze directly. "I know. And I promise if I need it, I'll say the safe word, but do your best. Make me beg."

The next thing she knew, she was flat on her back with Joe pinning her to the bed, his eyes blazing. Unable to help herself, she thrust her hips against his hard cock.

"You're mine, my delicate love slave."

She grinned at the lust and need in his voice, mildly surprised he called her his love slave, but then she remembered how he had reacted on the balcony when she whispered those very words to him. Exhilaration swept through her body. "Oh, please, don't tie me up." She half-heartedly struggled against him, playing with him. The fire in his eyes, so hot a few seconds ago, became a blazing inferno.

"No choice, my love slave." He clamped the velvet-covered restraint to her right wrist, then to the left. All the while his masculine fragrance teased her senses.

"I didn't mean to misbehave, m … Master." She hesitated over using the word. All her reading hadn't prepared her for what she was feeling with Joe. The good that came with being with the right person, someone who got you and didn't want to change you. God, just calling him Master had her pussy dripping.

"Is my delicate love slave afraid?" he asked, tenderness in his touch as he stroked her skin.

For a second she closed her eyes, letting the feel of his influence soak into every pore, every nerve. "Not afraid," she whispered when his fingers traced the curve of her neck. "Want more."

Talk about the ultimate fantasy. Vicki almost couldn't believe this was happening. She thought back to all those months she'd fantasized about Joe tying her up and fucking her senseless, and knew this was meant to be.

His palms brushed over her breasts, and she bucked her hips, trying to get him to hurry. "Be still, love slave." He tweaked her nipple, and she moaned in pleasure. He knew the right pressure to create pleasure instead of pain. He lowered his head and licked the valley between her breasts, then moved down and thrust his tongue into her belly button. Her hips jolted at the sweet sensation. "You're disobeying me," Joe said with mock anger.

"I'm sorry, Master, but I'm so hot for your hard cock." His teeth nipped her abdomen before going lower. Oh, Lord. His breath teased her pussy. She raised her hips on instinct, wanting him to strip off the thong and take her with his mouth.

"No, my lovely slave." His hands captured her hips, pressing her down. He slid the length of her body, one hand brushing against her pussy, before slipping to her inside thigh. Pure heat flowed over her body, as if she were burning up.

"Touch me, Master."

"I am." His fingers released her nylons from the garter. Keeping his fingers hooked around them, he ran his palms down her legs, past her knees and calves, until he could pull the stockings off. Then his fingers encircled her ankle. A slight tug and he had her right leg in the restraint, then he did the same to the left.

Vicki's breath caught in her throat. Cool air teased her pussy through the thong. She pulled against the restraints, only to find she was secured. She wouldn't be able to get away until he released her. Anticipation lodged in her throat.

The mattress dipped as Joe stood. Unabashed, she watched him undress. A whimper escaped her lips at the sight of his hard cock. Already the mushroom-shaped head was covered with pre-cum. "I want to taste you," she whispered. She needed to taste him, to take him deep in her mouth and make him explode.

He stared at her with raised eyebrows.

"Please, Master." She belatedly remembered her role in this fantasy.

"I'll think about it. I have other things I want to do first." He picked up a blindfold from the nightstand, then slipped it over her eyes, making sure it was secure but not tangled in her hair.

Vicki moaned at the loss of her sight. Could she handle this?

"It's okay, baby." His lips caressed her ear.

Yes, she could handle it. Joe would never hurt her. She took a deep breath and let it out.

"That's it. Concentrate on feeling, not on your sight. I want you to anticipate my touch, my lips, my cock. Not being able to see will heighten your other senses."

And it did. Already she was using her hearing to figure out what he was doing. The slight creak of the bed frame told her he had moved, then there was the smell of roses. The breath whooshed from her body as his palms covered her breasts and massaged oil into them. She thrust up into his hands, enjoying the feel of his fingers kneading her tender flesh.

"Feel what I'm doing. Know I'm watching your every reaction and know I can't wait to fuck you."

Vicki groaned as moisture slipped down her thighs. He was going to kill her.

Joe kept an eye on Vicki's face for any signs of distress. He wanted to make sure she was enjoying this, and from the look of pure ecstasy etched on her features, she was. Her body was flushed with excitement, and before he'd covered her eyes, he'd seen her anticipation. He wanted her to concentrate with all her other senses. Sound and smells had their place in arousing her. He loved the way her breasts swelled and her nipples peaked while he rubbed the rose-scented oil into her skin.

Reaching over, he picked up the nipple clamps. He began playing with her nipples, taking one between his thumb and forefinger, pinching it, tugging it until the rosy aureole elongated further. He paid attention to her swift intake of breath when he secured the first nipple clamp. "Okay?" he asked, gazing at her face for any signs of discomfort. He'd made sure the clamps were tight, but not enough to cause pain.

She nodded even as her fingers curled into her palms. He waited another moment, then proceeded to do the same with the other nipple. With every movement her breathing became more ragged.

"Do you know how sexy you look, spread eagle in front of me, your nipples in my clamps, begging for me to play with them?"

Sweat beaded on his forehead. Damn, he was going to have a difficult time holding off. His body clamored for him to take her, hard and fast. But he would wait. There was so much more pleasure he wanted to give her. He flicked the clamps, and she let out a loud moan. "Don't make too much noise, baby, we don't want the neighbors calling hotel security, do we?"

She shook her head. Next, he picked up the fur-covered mitt and slipped it over his hand. When he placed it on her belly, she jumped.

"Easy." He moved his hand in a circular motion. "How does it feel?"

"Soft. Comforting. Damn sensuous." Her head shook from side to side on the bed.

Slowly, he caressed her with the fur mitt, enjoying the way she reacted to him. The flush on her skin deepened, followed by goose bumps as he continued to run the mitt over her body. Her legs stiffened as he stroked her inner thigh, then her calf, down to her ankle, and over the bottoms of her feet.

A giggle escaped her, and he smiled in the knowledge she was ticklish. So endearing and human. Lifting his hand, he skimmed up her arm before caressing her breasts, enjoying how they strained into his touch before he stopped.

Her thong was soaked with her desire. His cock demanded attention. It wept for the relief only her hot pussy could give him, but still he held back. This wasn't just about him. This was a sensual journey for them both.

Still, he felt like a teenager hot for his first woman. Removing the mitt, he picked up the next item and nestled between her thighs. Her legs stiffened once again, but then relaxed when he touched her waist. "Remember what I said earlier about this thong?" Without waiting for a response, Joe gripped the fabric and gave a jerk. The flimsy material snapped. He eased it away from her body and threw it across the room.

He glanced up at Vicki. Her mouth was open and she was panting. Her breasts quivered with every breath she took. A good sign. He prepared himself for the next task. Using his fingers, he spread her pussy lips. Her clit peeked out from its hood—hard, pink, and begging for his attention. He'd attached a small vibrator to his tongue and turned it on, so each time he licked her, the buzzing stimulated her clit.

"Oh, shit," she cried out, hips arching toward him. He raised his head. Then with a grin, he licked her again. She didn't cry out this time, but it didn't stop her hips from bucking.

He teased her with short licks until her juices flowed, then his mouth covered her clit, and he plunged two fingers into her dripping channel. When her hips arched this time, he was ready. He grabbed the pillow he'd set nearby and slipped it beneath her, keeping her pelvis tilted and against his mouth. He began loving her with his tongue and fingers, devouring her sweet juices.

Vicki thought she was going insane. The vibrator against her clit sent such delicious sensations through her body, and Joe's fingers in her pussy made her clench with need. And when he put the pillow beneath her hips … she cried out in ecstasy. The sensations coursing through her body made her so sensitive and alive. Her sex pressed against his lips as he moved his tongue around, pushing the vibrator to caress her entire clit. She was helpless against her body's reaction.

She could feel her juices running freely. Her breasts were swelling, and she knew from the heat coursing through her body they were probably rosy as well. Hell, her whole body was on fire. And her nipples, even with the clamps on them, were straining for more attention.

Her fingers curled into fists before straightening once again. She wanted to touch him, to run her fingers through his dark hair, to hold him against her. But she couldn't. Never had a man made her feel this way. Out of control. Out of control and loving every second of it. She didn't have to worry about anyone but herself, and it was all because of Joe. He took his time with her, prepared her body to accept him, and made her want him. But it was more—he enjoyed exploring his sensuality as well as hers.

Her hips bucked again when he moved his fingers deep within her channel. The sound of wet suction from his movements inflamed her senses. Oh, God, she was so close to coming. Her belly muscles clenched and Joe seemed to sense it. He moved his tongue and fingers. Faster. Harder.

No. She wanted to yell, *not yet!* But she had no control at all. The sweet pressure built and built until she exploded. Only at the last second did she remember to bite her lip to stop herself from screaming. She didn't want people in the next room or anywhere in the hotel to hear her and call the front desk or, worse, the police. There was no way she was going to give up this night, not for any reason.

Tiny sounds of pleasure escaped her lips anyway. Her body trembled with the force of her orgasm. And, Joe, damn him, never stopped loving her until her butt dropped against the pillow in exhaustion.

The mattress moved, then a smacking sound rang out—he'd just licked her juices from his lips. Her pussy ached for him once again. Her ears strained to hear any little sound, but all she made out was her own ragged breathing. What did he have planned for her now? She squirmed in anticipation.

Joe smiled down at Vicki. She had no idea of how beautiful she looked at this moment. Her body gleamed with the afterglow of her climax, yet showed signs of new arousal as she waited for his next action.

Quietly, he reached over and removed one of the nipple clamps, and his lips closed over the distended flesh as she cried out in pleasure. He rolled his tongue around the nub, soothing it until her moans quieted. Then he did the same with the other. When he lifted his head, she let out a sigh.

She was squirming on the bed, her breathing erratic. And from the way she was wiggling against the sheets, she was nearing completion again. Good, that's where he wanted her. With deliberate action, he let the clamps fall from his hand and clatter onto the table. Her body tensed, then relaxed. Oh, she wouldn't be so relaxed in a minute. He grinned as he leaned down and blew air against her nipple.

"Ah!" Her back bowed, her hips rose, but the restraints hampered her. The pillow beneath her hips restricted her movements even more. She was at his mercy. Power and gratitude filled him.

He stroked his hard cock. For a moment he was tempted to jerk himself off just for the relief it would give him. But no, he would hold back. It would heighten his senses to delay his own climax. It wouldn't be easy, but he would do it for her, for his Vicki. He wanted to give his pleasure as well as her own.

Turning, he grabbed another item off the table. The bed dipped as he moved between her thighs once again. Her musky scent teased him, making his cock twitch and pre-cum flow. *Soon. Soon, I'll sink into her sweet wet channel and have my way with her, but not yet.*

Lying down, he used his left hand to open her pussy lips, and then in his right he took the feather and tickled her clit.

"Oh, God, Joe," she cried out, her body convulsing from the light touch.

"I didn't give you permission to come again, love slave." He set the feather down and lightly slapped her thigh, and she squirmed.

"I'm sorry, Master, but your love slave needs your big hard cock in her."

His prick jumped at her words. He needed her too, but … An

idea formed. He was strong enough to carry it off as long as he was careful. "As you wish," he whispered, then positioned himself. His cock was above her luscious lips while he faced her feet. He wanted to tickle her with the feather at the same time as she pleasured him. "You will suck me, love slave, and you will not climax."

Joe placed the feather between his teeth, braced his hands against the mattress, adjusted his feet, and lowered his cock to her mouth. The tip of his dick nudged her lips, and she opened them, enveloping his penis. Joe dropped his head and moved the feather over her breasts.

Her cry of surprise sent vibrations through his cock, then she began sucking him. Her tongue swirled around the tip of his cock, coaxing more fluid from him. He struggled not to face-fuck her. That would be for another time; right now he wanted her pleasure to come first. Instead, he traced the feather over her nipples, her breasts, her belly, and the outer folds of her pussy. She squirmed and wiggled, but she never stopped sucking him. He concentrated on his job and not on how sweet her lips and tongue were on his dick.

Joe enjoyed the way her body flushed at his sensual play, but when she took him completely into her mouth, it was his turn to groan. Gritting his teeth around the shaft that held the feather, he gathered his strength. This was going to be a test of wills. Who would come first? Not him. He clenched the feather tighter, then he rotated it over her glistening folds, teasing her labia until her body shook. Then he went in for the kill. He let the feather slip from his mouth and lowered his head.

She cried out around his cock when he closed his mouth over her pussy. He drew her straining clit into his mouth and started sucking. Only a minute elapsed before she exploded.

Satisfaction never tasted so good. He brought her to another climax: a few more to go. Bracing himself, he started to pull his cock from her slack mouth. Her teeth scraped along his skin, and he almost sank back down into her warm, willing mouth. He shook his head. This was meant for her, for both of them. Her pleasure meant everything to him.

When he climbed off the bed, she called his name in a soft voice filled with need. His control almost broke. She sounded so desperate, so ... He couldn't describe it. She wasn't quite begging him, more like pleading with him. "Shhh." He brushed a kiss against her damp forehead, then repositioned himself so he could kiss his way down her body. Once he reached her feet, he removed the ankle restraints. Then he moved to the head of the bed. "I'm going to release your wrist restraints for a moment. You're not to touch the blindfold, but roll onto your stomach."

"Yes, Master," she whispered.

Within seconds, he had the restraints off. He waited until she lay flat on her stomach, the pillow beneath her hips, which raised her ass high. Then he re-secured her wrists. He looked at her incredible butt and ran his hands over the pale globes. She shivered. "You climaxed a second time without permission."

"I know, Master." There was no regret in her voice, only satisfaction.

"And does the Master's love slave know how she's going to be punished?"

"With pleasure."

The hopeful tone in her voice caused Joe to laugh. He couldn't help it. She constantly surprised him. "Yes, with pleasure." He dipped his fingers between her thighs, caressing her briefly. "But first, I think you need to be taught a lesson." He brought his palm down on her ass as he plunged two fingers into her pussy.

"Ouch," she cried out, but Joe knew it was more from surprise than pain. He wasn't into pain, but titillation, anticipation, and sensuality.

She wiggled her hips. "You must ask for my permission to come, do you understand me, love slave?" He swatted her ass again.

"Yes, Master," was her quick answer, her pelvis pressed against his fingers.

He spanked her a few more times, all the while teasing her with his fingers. He was having a hard time containing himself. Her moans of pleasure made his body shake with need. She turned him on like no other woman, and he couldn't hold out any longer. "Your ass is rosy from my hand and your pussy is dripping. How do you feel?"

"Hot and … "

He waited, but she only panted, not saying another word. "And what?" His palm descended once again, and he twisted his fingers inside her pussy.

Another groan left her lips. "I need your cock, Master. I need you to fuck me. I want to come so bad, but when I do, I want you in me. Fuck me. Please, fuck me." The need, the want, the desire in her voice caused his prick to swell.

He pulled his fingers out of her channel and placed them on her hips. "On your knees." His voice was husky as he gave her the command. With his help, she was able to get to her knees, ass up in the air, her forehead against the mattress. Kneeling behind her, Joe positioned himself. He cursed.

"Joe?"

"I forgot the condom." He held still, trying to find the strength to leave her heat and get the rubber.

"It's okay. I'm protected."

Those were the words he needed to hear. He curled his fingers around her hips and with one thrust buried himself deep inside her. A groan left his lips.

"Joe!" She cried out his name in pleasure.

"I promised you I'd bury my cock on the first thrust." Her

hot, moist pussy enveloped him, and he had to fight not to shift. He wanted to give her time to adjust to his quick invasion. He wanted her to feel how hard she made him, and he wanted to savor her tightness.

"How does my dick feel, love slave?" He rotated his hips and she whimpered.

"Hard, blazing, and delicious." She paused and he imagined her tongue darting out to moisten her lips. "Fuck me, Master."

"All in good time." He was buried in her, his control almost restored. He wanted to tease her some more. Keeping his hands on her hips, holding her in place, he pulled back in a slow measured stroke. She tightened around him, trying to keep him from escaping. Then he slid back in. He did it again and again, all in agonizing slowness, fighting his own urges to take her hard and fast. She felt so good under him, around him. He wanted to take his time, to enjoy her and make her want him even more.

Vicki's breathing became more ragged. With Joe holding onto her hips, she wasn't able to thrust against him or increase his pace. And with her hands restrained, she couldn't use them for leverage. "Don't tease me anymore," she yelled, when he slid into her for the fifth time. Didn't he realize he was driving her crazy?

"I will do what I want," he replied between clenched teeth. Yeah, he would. He slid his fingers across her stomach to her clit.

Her body bucked against his at the sensation of his running his nail over her clit. He pulled out, then slid back in, still in slow motion. *Oh, God.* This was killing her. She needed him, and if he kept playing with her, she was going to come without his permission. And she didn't want to disappoint Joe by doing so. "Damn it, Joe. Will you please fuck me?" She all but shouted the words.

He chuckled. "Hold on, baby, I might get a little rough."

"I don't care. Fuck me. Fuck me hard. Fuck me fast, but just fuck me!" Her control was shattered and she didn't care. She wanted Joe. All of him. Vicki groaned when he pulled back slowly, then sank into her with the same agonizing slowness. "Damn it." She tried to thrust back against him, but he had her trapped and she was unable to do much. "Will you move faster?"

He was teasing the hell out of her with this slow penetration. She wanted him, hard, fast, and deep, so deep she'd be able to feel him against her womb. Her fingers curled into her palms, and her knuckles ached. With the blindfold still covering her eyes, she couldn't see. All she could do was feel. And damn it, she was feeling. Every vein on his cock teased the insides of her pussy. There was more. Joe's ragged breathing reached her ears, along with an occasional groan. And … she couldn't explain it. There was an invisible thread between them, connecting their hearts, minds, and bodies. A sense of peace and belonging stole over her heart.

Her clit throbbed as his fingers brushed over it. A shiver ran all the way through her body. *Shit!* She was going to come if he wasn't careful. "Come on, Joe, move," she ordered.

"I think you've forgotten who's in charge." His voice was gruff.

Her ass stung for a moment when he swatted her. She ground her teeth together. Oh, God, she couldn't take this for much longer without coming. Already, her stomach was tightening. She fought to keep her orgasm in check. *Think of something, anything! Stop concentrating on how he's making you feel.* Nothing worked. She inhaled through her nose. Time to pay the piper. "You're in charge, Master," she whispered, hoping to spur him into fucking her.

"Good answer, love slave." His voice was soft. Then he pressed his lips against her spine. He moved a tad faster, but not fast enough. She needed him to fuck her—now. He pressed the pad of his finger against her clit, creating a delicious electric sensation to echo through her body. It wasn't enough to make her come, but it kept her arousal high. She had to do something; she was dying here.

"Please, Master." Her breathing was shallow and it was difficult to get the words out. "Your love slave needs your cock, she needs your seed filling her. Please, Master, fuck your love slave." Damn, her own words were arousing her even more. She bit back a moan when he stopped moving, his cock filling her pussy to the brim. Her juices ran down the inside of her thighs.

"Who do you belong to, love slave?" His voice was husky.

"You, Master," she answered without hesitation. She belonged to Joe and no one else. A band snapped inside of her, making her world whole and beautiful.

"Right answer." He pulled out and then thrust into her.

Yes! Her mind cried out as he pistoned in and out of her. She groaned as he thrust. "Yes, Master. Fuck your love slave, show her who's the boss." God, she wanted this. Needed this. Needed to feel his control, his mastery over her body, and his love.

She should be shocked at her own words, but she wasn't This was Joe, the man she'd been waiting for all her life. He was so hard, so big. She loved every inch of him. She panted, trying to get more air into her lungs as her climax began to rise.

Joe must have realized it, because he flicked his finger over her clit harder and faster.

Yes, yes, yes! She screamed as her orgasm hit. Her body trembled with the force of it. God, he felt so good inside her. Her pussy clenched around him.

After what seemed like an hour, she was able to breathe again. She realized Joe was still deep within her, his cock rock hard. "You forgot to ask permission again, love slave." Amusement tinged his voice.

Oh, fuck. Vicki groaned as Joe moved once again—slowly,

deliberately. She wanted to pound her fists against the mattress, but couldn't. "I can't take any more," she whispered, her body tightened to his leisurely strokes. It just wasn't fair.

"Yes, you can." He stopped moving and pressed against her. His body shifted to her right, and then there was a noise. He was fumbling for something on the table.

A shiver swept through her at the thought of what he was going to do to her next. She held her breath, listening for any clue. Nothing. The pressure against her lessened, and he once again moved at a lazy pace.

How could he have so much control over his body and hers? Not fair that he could hold back his climax. She wanted to make him come.

When he pushed into her, she tightened her pussy. Joe groaned. She did it again and again, her smile widening with each groan he gave.

"Is my love slave trying to make her master come?" he asked in a velvety voice against her spine. The deep rumble sent vibrations through her body.

She didn't answer, only concentrated on tightening those muscles once again. She loved the feel of him filling her, stretching her, pulsing within her pussy.

"Oh, you're only making things worse."

Before she could even think about what his words meant, his fingers spread her pussy lips wide. Her chest pressed harder against the mattress as her back arched into him. He was creating more friction between them, but, no, there was something more. Something cool and round pressed against her clit.

"Are you ready for a wild ride, my love slave?" he asked, before pulling back and slamming his cock inside her. At the same time, something pulsed on her clit. Damn it, he had a vibrating bullet! She couldn't fight her own orgasm any longer, not with that deliciously wicked device tormenting her. She screamed as an unexpected climax ripped through her.

Joe didn't stop. This time he kept fucking her. "That's it, baby," he whispered. "Come for me, feel me within you, fucking you. Fucking you hard and harder yet. I'm going to make you come and then you'll come some more."

Vicki couldn't believe she was on edge, again, already. It was as if someone else had taken over her body. The buzzing became louder as Joe increased the bullet's speed. She bucked against his body. She wasn't going to be able to hold out much longer. Already another orgasm was building.

"Oh, yes, my love slave. I can feel your next climax rising." He thrust faster. "No, don't fight it. I want you to come. I want to feel your juices around my cock, on my fingers. I want to see them dripping onto the sheets."

Even with the knowledge her orgasm was coming, it surprised her with its force. And there was another one right behind it. Then another. "Joe," she cried out as he turned up the vibrations on the bullet once again.

"Yes, love slave, I'm here. Fucking you. Making you come."

"I can't … " She gasped for air. She considered using the safe word, then discarded it. Joe hadn't come yet. And damned if she would give up until he climaxed. She wanted him to feel pleasure since he'd given her so much.

"If it's too much, say the safe word, baby, and I'll stop."

The damn man could read her mind. She shook her head. "I can take it." At least she hoped she could. Her body was so sensitive. So *alive*. All her nerve endings tingled.

"Yes, you can." The admiration in his voice made her pride swell, then he did the impossible. He thrust harder and faster, and turned the damn bullet up another notch. Her body convulsed once again, her juices dripping down her legs, and she was sure onto the sheets as well, just as he'd said he wanted. Another orgasm began rising. Panting, she arched her back further, her head thrashing from side to side as her body continued to shake. "Just one more, baby. This one will blow us both apart."

He turned the bullet on high and she screamed into the mattress. Her butt pressed up against him as he thrust into her one last time. Her body shook as her pussy continued to pulse and tighten around his cock. Her orgasm kept coming even as his cock twitched as he spilled his seed.

Just as her climax waned, another one hit, harder, and she couldn't stop her body this time. She trembled in his arms, forcing her hips higher as if she wanted to swallow his cock and balls within her. The bullet against her clit drove her release to new levels. The vibrations spread through her body, and her last thought was she'd never find this with another man, didn't want to, then blackness claimed her.

Vicki slumped in his arms. Damn. He turned the vibrator off and tossed it to the floor, then withdrew from her pulsing body. "Vicki," he whispered. He'd never forgive himself if he'd hurt her. He unfastened her wrists, ripped off the blindfold, and cradled her body against his.

"Hmm ... "

"Baby, are you all right?" he asked, kissing her temple.

"Uh-huh." Her lashes fluttered upward, and he was able to see into her eyes. They were filled with passion, satisfaction, and exhaustion.

Relief surged through him. She was okay. "Be right back." He dropped a kiss on her lips, lay her down on the bed, and stood. After going into the bathroom, Joe turned on the faucet, tested the temperature, and made adjustments until it was below hot. Then he watched the water fill the tub. A bath was in order for both of them. Going back into the bedroom, Joe noticed Vicki hadn't moved. Lifting her into his arms, his heart filled with pleasure as she curled against his body. The weight and warmth of her felt so right.

"So tired," she whispered.

"You can sleep soon." He stepped into the tub, and lowered them both into the steaming water.

She was all but purring in his arms as the water closed over their bodies. "This is nice," she murmured.

"Yes, it is." He wanted to give her everything she needed and then some.

He made short work of their bath and dried them both off as Vicki all but fell asleep on her feet. After carrying her back to bed, he lay her down, covering her with the sheet and blanket before joining her.

Leaning on one elbow, he gazed down at her serene face, and inhaled the lingering sweet aroma from the hotel soap. He'd finally found the woman he wanted to spend the rest of his life with. A woman he loved with all his heart.

Chapter Eight

Vicki woke the next morning to the delicious sensation of having Joe's body draped over hers. Well, almost. His arm was around her waist, his legs entangled with hers, and his breath teased the skin of her neck. She'd never felt so contented, so secure in her life. But as much as she wanted to stay there and savor these feelings, Mother Nature called.

After carefully extricating herself from Joe's embrace, she made her way into the bathroom. Once she'd finished, she pulled on a robe and padded out to the main room. First things first: check out what time they needed to be downstairs for the conference, and then order breakfast. Tapping her finger against her lips, she smiled. Breakfast in bed sounded like a good idea.

As she reached for the phone, she noticed an envelope on the floor near the door. Going over to it, she reached down, picked it up, and turned it over. Her heart stuttered. With shaking fingers, she opened the flap and pulled out the single sheet of paper. The familiar handwriting jumped out at her as she read the words: *I know what you did on the balcony, slut. You're mine.*

Derek. He was here, now. She stood there with the letter in a shaking hand. She'd attributed all the so-called 'sightings' she'd had to nerves, but now she had to wonder. Yes, he could have followed her and Joe, but there was no way he'd know for sure what happened on the balcony.

Oh, it was easy to make the supposition, but she didn't care what Derek thought any more. With an angry sigh, she slipped the paper back into the envelope. Should she call the police? She hadn't gotten the restraining order yet. Would they be able to do anything? If Derek continued his stalking the justice system would take care of him—he was the past. Joe was her future. A weight lifted from her shoulders knowing she had Joe in her corner.

Turning, she found Joe lounging against the bedroom door, his blue eyes sleepy yet glowing with satisfaction. He was nude. "Now, that's a good morning view," she said as she pushed the envelope into the pocket of her robe and shoved all thoughts of Derek out of her mind. She wasn't going to spoil her time with Joe.

Joe crossed the room, and his lips claimed hers. Hot waves swept through her body as she entwined her arms around his neck. No more hiding. It was time for her to be the woman she wanted to be. Joe wasn't afraid of her sensuality—he reveled in it. Their lips parted. "It's a good morning now," he whispered before his tongue teased her earlobe.

"I thought we might have breakfast in bed."

"Good idea." He swept her into his arms.

"Joe!" She was too heavy for him to be lifting her, yet he did with ease. She leaned into his strong chest.

"Did I forget to tell you? I want *you* for breakfast." His mouth closed over hers once again, and she forgot everything except how he made her feel so loved.

THE NEXT TWO days they spent in a series of lectures, and the nights were spent loving each other. The morning she had received the note, Vicki kept a careful lookout for Derek, but never set eyes on him. She decided anyone could have written that note. After all, she and Joe hadn't been totally discreet. Anyone could jump to the conclusion of what they'd been doing.

She'd called the detective in charge of her case. He'd advised her to keep her eyes open, but without the restraining order, the New Orleans Police couldn't do much. But she was to bring the note back so he could add it to the file.

The emotional wound Derek caused had healed, thanks to Joe's loving care.

Glancing up, she spied Joe talking with one of the vendors. She had found it increasingly difficult the past few days to be businesslike during the time they spent at the conference. There were occasions when she wanted nothing more than to yank him into her arms and kiss him until neither of them could breathe, but he had promised to keep it cool during business hours, so she had to do the same.

If only her body would quit throbbing with the need to be in his arms, to feel his caress, to have him take her. She shifted from one foot to the other. This morning, Joe had made love to her with such tenderness she still felt the impact of it. Not their usual frantic hot sex, but she didn't mind it slow. She loved everything Joe did to her body. Tilting her head, she stared at him, enjoying the way his suit jacket stretched over his wide shoulders.

Her gaze roamed down to his hands. Large palms that had cradled her with affection after they made love, fingers that made her scream out with passion as they fucked.

And he made her feel … Her heart stopped beating. He made her feel safe, secure, sexy, not to mention wild and lovable. Vicki took a deep breath. *I'm in love.* The thought came out of the blue. Instead of the ever-present fear, she was calm. Well, maybe not.

I'm in love with Joe Bradshaw.

A tingling started through her body, making her feel even

more alive than before. Her heart was telling her Joe was nothing like Derek. Joe might be a commanding and forceful man, but he wasn't possessive like Derek, and he would never hit her or intentionally hurt her with words. Joe was a good man, and deep down she'd known it from the beginning. Her own fear had kept her from acknowledging it so she wouldn't fall in love with him. But she had. And when they flew home, the day after tomorrow, she was going to do everything in her power to keep this relationship with him.

"Ready?" Joe asked, cupping her elbow.

Vicki blinked, so lost in her thoughts she hadn't realized he had finished his conversation and crossed to her side. "Ready for what?"

"I was thinking dinner in the French Quarter."

"Sounds delicious."

"Let's go change."

Heat flared as he guided her across the lobby to the elevators. How was she going to survive dinner without jumping his bones? Once they were inside their room, she turned and curled her arms around his neck. "We're not working now."

He didn't resist when she drew his lips down to hers. Her tongue dove into his mouth, tasting the dark coffee he'd drunk just an hour ago. She started to deepen the kiss when he eased her away from him.

"Hey," she protested, but his heavy breathing filled the air. He was just as affected as she was.

"Dinner, then we can continue this." His expression was tight, as if he were fighting back his own desire.

"What if I want to continue this now?" Her wild side was free, and it relished being with a man who enjoyed her kinkiness.

His blue eyes turned dark with desire as her hand found the bulge in his crotch. She caressed him through the fabric. "Vicki, please." His palms rested on her wrist, preventing her from stroking him.

"I want to please you," she whispered, nibbling kisses across his chin. "I so want to please you, Joe." Her hand tightened around his cock.

He groaned and his hips flexed, pushing into her palm. A flash of intense pleasure and power shot through her body.

Raising her arm, she started to push off his jacket. Dinner could wait. "Let's get naked and try out the bathroom counter." His gaze flare even hotter as he fought for control. But she didn't want him in control. She wanted him wild, as wild as she felt.

His jacket slid off his shoulders, part of it pooling around his left wrist as he still held her right arm. She tightened her fingers around his cock and another groan left his mouth. He released her wrist and the jacket fell to the floor. "Witch," he muttered.

Nipping his earlobe, she unfastened his shirt with one hand. His fingers were already unzipping the back of her dress. Seconds later they were both naked and their hot, heavy breathing filled the air.

Vicki ran her nails over his chest, teasing his nipples, before moving lower. His abdomen tightened when her palm passed over. Then her left hand joined her right, cupping him, and he grew larger within her grasp. "I love how you feel," she said against his skin, kissing her way down his body before falling to her knees. "And you smell so good. Musky and masculine." Her tongue darted out and she licked the head of his cock, tasting his unique flavor. His body shuddered and she hid a smile. Leaning back, she glanced up. He was staring at her, but his hands were clenched at his side.

Time to make him lose control.

"Do you like this?" She took him deep into her mouth, sucking, before releasing him. He grasped her shoulders, urging her up. She rose to her feet, tilted her head, and studied his face. Passion was evident in his eyes, but there were lines creasing his forehead. "Don't you want—" Her words were cut off when he placed his fingers against her lips. She drew one into her mouth and sucked.

A feral glaze clouded his eyes. "I want you more than anything in the world." His words escaped from between clenched teeth.

"But," she mumbled around his digits.

"Don't say a thing." His fingers left her mouth with a *pop* before he kissed her, hard and hot.

Before she realized what was happening, she was in his arms and in the bathroom. With a sweep of his arm, he sent everything clattering to the floor. The cool tile against her butt caused goose bumps to appear all over, but it only lasted a second until his hands cupped her ass, moving her closer to the edge as he stepped between her knees.

Her mouth fell open in a gasp, and she grabbed his shoulders when he thrust inside her to the hilt on the first stroke. He was hot, hard and … He pulled out and did it again. "Joe," she cried out, her back arching, bringing them closer yet.

"You're so wet." His hands caressed her ass, holding her against him for a moment. Then he pulled his cock out before thrusting home again. Her internal muscles tightened with each thrust.

"I love how you make me feel when you're fucking me." The words came out slowly as she fought to breathe and talk at the same time.

"I love the way you take me all the way into your body." His pace increased.

"Yes!" Her nails dug into his shoulders. "That's it, Joe, fuck me. Lose control and give it all to me." She pushed her hips forward, meeting him thrust for thrust. When his fingers found her clit, her climax exploded.

His hands were beneath her ass, keeping her body plastered against his. Panting, she lay her forehead on his shoulder while she continued to pulse around him. After a few minutes, she realized two things. He was still deep inside her, and he was still hard.

Turning her head, she tasted the saltiness of his sweaty skin. He captured her mouth. His tongue tangled with hers as he lifted her.

She tore her mouth away. "Joe?" What was he up to? Mischief played around his lips and his eyes shone brighter, causing a shiver of excitement to run through her body.

"Let's see, we still have two walls, in front of the balcony windows, the chair, and … "He licked the rim of her ear. "Someone mentioned last night several different positions she wanted to try."

A small laugh emerged. Leave it to him to remember her words whispered in the heat of passion. She didn't mind. "Are you up to it, lover?" She shifted her hips, and his eyes darkened.

"More than you think, my love."

And he proved it to her, over and over again.

JOE SLIPPED OUT of bed the next morning with a grin on his face. Vicki was still sound asleep. He didn't expect anything else, not after the night they'd had. His body tightened at the memories.

Grabbing a robe, he slid it on and sauntered out of the room to call room service. Today was their last day in New Orleans. The conference would end by seven, and he wanted to plan a special night in celebration of their relationship.

He meandered over to the window and looked out, lost in thought until a knock sounded. Crossing the room, he pulled open the door. "What's this?" he asked the room service waiter, who carried a long white box.

"Sorry, sir. The box was sitting outside the door. I figured you'd want them inside."

Joe nodded. Who was sending Vicki flowers? Who was this unknown suitor? His gut tightened. After signing the bill and adding a tip, he shut the door and frowned. Was there something familiar about the waiter? Crossing the room back to where the box sat by their covered food, an uneasy feeling flowed through his body.

"Oh, good, coffee, I need … " Vicki emerged from their bedroom, her hair mussed and her face bright. She stopped talking when she noticed the box. "Flowers, you shouldn't have."

"I didn't." *Trust.* He trusted her. She wasn't a woman who would fool around on him. Hell, there hadn't been time.

"Then who?" She lifted the lid. The box slipped from her fingers, and black roses cascaded around her.

"What the fuck?" He pulled her into his embrace when she swayed on her feet. Her green gaze clashed with his. Her face was so pale he was afraid she was going to pass out. Pushing his anger aside for the moment, he guided her over to the sofa and sat her down before going back and pouring her a cup of coffee. "Take a sip or two."

He placed the cup to her lips, the liquid flowing into her mouth before she grimaced. "Too sweet."

"It will help." He sat, his arm automatically curving around her shoulders. Silence filled the room before she sighed and set the cup of coffee down. "Want to tell me who would send you black roses?" he asked. Black roses meant death. And as much as he wanted to slay all her dragons, he couldn't do so until he knew who or what he was dealing with.

"Derek," she whispered.

Her words held him silent for a second. Was there more to the story than she had already told him? "Tell me the entire story?"

"Derek became a little … possessive." Her body shook and Joe tightened his arm around her, pulling her against his body. She gave a sigh and relaxed. "Possessive isn't the right word. He was jealous of everyone I came into contact with, and he wanted nothing more than to control my life. Of course, I didn't realize this at first. I brushed off his attitude as just wanting us to be alone, but after we moved in together I couldn't ignore it any longer. Not after … "

"Vicki." Joe couldn't stand the pain he was seeing her eyes. It cut him to the bone.

She brought her hand up and cupped his cheek, coolness against his warm skin. "I want you to know so we can move on. I should have told you the whole story before now." She drew her lower lip between her teeth, worrying at it before releasing it. "I lived with Derek for three months and realized I had made a mistake after the first week. A foolish mistake. When I tried to break it off, he … " Her lashes fell and she tucked her head beneath his chin.

Several things ran through his mind, from his abusing her, to rape, to … but then all the pieces fell into place. How she had flinched in a meeting when one of the other managers slammed his hand on the table. "He hit you."

"Yes," she whispered.

"He's a dead man." His voice was ice cold.

She closed her hand over his clenched fist. "No, Joe." The fierceness of her voice and the gentleness of her touch brought him back to earth. She gazed up at him with trust in those lush green eyes.

"He hurt you." His lips nudged a strand of hair away from her face, brushing a kiss against her temple.

"I won't lie, he hurt me. But only once. I walked out the same night."

"But you're still afraid of him." He'd seen her reaction to those roses. The fear, the loathing.

"Not anymore." She wiggled against his body, as if finding a more comfortable spot before continuing. "The roses surprised me. You see, when I dated before, the guys I was seeing wouldn't call after the first date and I didn't understand why. It was Derek. He bragged to me about threatening the men who showed an interest in me."

The notes he'd been getting now added up. He'd dismissed them, but not anymore. "So you kept pushing me away because of him." More pieces of the puzzle fell into place, and he didn't like the picture it was making.

She grimaced. "Yes, but I realized you were stronger than all those other men. I decided yesterday I need to get Derek out of my life for good. When we get back to Seattle, I'm going to file a police report."

Shock stilled him. "He's been stalking you."

"Yes." She blew out a breath. "I'm embarrassed by the whole thing. I stopped dating, hoping he'd just go away."

"But that didn't happen, did it?" He rubbed her back, hoping to soothe her rattled nerves.

"No. He started calling me and sending me notes. I thought I kept seeing him around, but when I looked there was no one there. I chalked it up to nerves." She glanced up at him, her cheeks red.

"Honey, you have nothing to be embarrassed about." He saw the waiter in his mind's eye and frowned.

"What does he look like?"

"Brown hair, skinny, shorter than you, pretty nondescript."

Except the description matched the waiter and possibly the guy he'd caught sight of the other day outside the women's bathroom. He didn't want to alarm Vicki, so he kept his tone neutral as he asked, "Have you filed any police reports yet?"

"I've talked with them. The officer started a case file last week, and I'm in the process of getting a restraining order."

"Why didn't you file a police report before now?" He was curious why she hadn't.

Her shoulder moved in a shrug. "I honestly figured he'd give up. I never answered his calls, and I guess deep down inside I wanted to believe he'd forget about me and move on. Plus, the police on the phone said there wasn't much they could do since Derek hadn't approached or threatened me." She took a deep breath. "But since you've come into my life, I've realized how much time I've wasted over Derek. I wanted him out of my life and going to the police station was the first step. I refuse to let him affect me anymore, especially since I have you. You've shown me I can be the woman I want to be without fear."

Of all the things he'd expected to hear, this wasn't it. She was a woman of extraordinary courage. She'd walked out on her abuser, and now she trusted him. It humbled him. He lowered his lips and brushed a soft kiss against her mouth. Lifting his head, he gazed down at her. "When we get back to Seattle, we'll tackle Derek together. You don't have to face this alone."

She sagged against his. "Sounds nice." Then her stomach let out a growl.

They laughed, and the sound lifted the oppressive feeling in the room.

"I think someone is hungry," Joe teased.

"Yes. Food, please."

"Your wish is my command, my dearest love." The words didn't shock him. She was his love.

VICKI PAUSED AT the entrance to the banquet room later in the evening. Joe hadn't left her side all night, but she'd finally convinced him to give her a few minutes in the ladies' room and promised she'd meet him at the bar. Tonight was their last night in New Orleans, and she was going to have a blast. Spying Joe paying for their drinks at the bar, she took a step toward him when a hand clamped down on her shoulder.

"Hello, Victoria."

Derek's cold voice raced down her spine with a chilling effect. Turning her head, her gaze collided with his lethal one.

Oh, shit. His face was tight, his brown hair mussed, and his eyes wild. Her heart leapt into her throat. She'd been so convinced Derek was playing her from a distance, she'd let her guard down. She backed away, clutching the air behind her, trying to find something to hold on to. "Derek." His name fell from her lips, weighted with dread. She struggled to remain composed without her body freezing in shock. All the while, his stone-cold eyes bored into hers. There was no escaping him. The door jamb bit into her palms.

He came closer. She could smell his breath. He'd been drinking. "You're coming with me," he snarled. "I've had it with your shit." His grip on her shoulder tightened, becoming painful. She wanted to wrench herself free, but he dragged her from the doorway.

"Let me go." She tried to shrug away his hold, but it didn't work. Instead, she bent her knees, and his fingers slipped as she tried to duck aside. He snagged her around the waist. "Let me go!" She struggled with him as he pulled her back against his body.

"Don't make a scene, Victoria," Derek whispered, his breath hot and foul. "You better start acting like my wife." A hacking gurgle she could only interpret as laughter accompanied his words.

She tried to break free again, tears filling her eyes at the pain of her forearm twisting in his grasp. He managed to get her in front of him. His heavy breathing ruffled her hair as Derek frog-marched her down the hall and toward a door. Fear began to overwhelm her. Going limp in his arms, she forced him to drag her, and in the process she lost one of her shoes.

JOE GLANCED OVER at the door again, then back at his watch, then back at the door. Ten minutes had passed. Vicki wouldn't keep him waiting longer than necessary.

"Did you see that man and woman out in the hall?" said a girl to her friend as they sauntered up to the bar.

"Yeah," said the friend, "he looked a bit dangerous."

Derek. Vicki.

"Call security!" Joe didn't wait for a response. He took off running. He heard Vicki's voice, saw her shoe on the floor and then a flash of brown down the hallway as a door closed ahead of him. Joe ran down the hall and burst through the door onto a loading dock to find Vicki struggling with Derek as he wrestled her toward the ramp to a car.

Fear rushed through Joe's bloodstream. Not fear for him, but for Vicki. Derek was dangerous, more than she thought. Vicki struggled with Derek, trying to get free. He only had seconds to come up with a plan to save the woman he loved.

Vicki took a deep breath, then raked her nails over the back of Derek's hand and stomped on his foot. She spun out of his hold, but wasn't fast enough to get any real space between them. His hand tangled in her hair.

"Bitch. You're going to pay." He raised his fist.

Vicki braced herself for the blow.

"Let her go. Now!" His order rang through the silence.

She gave a cry of relief. Joe's voice was like sweet music to her ears.

"Go away, this doesn't concern you." Derek's tone was dismissive.

Tears slid from the corners of her eyes when he pulled her back to him by her hair. Her gaze collided with Joe's. Her heart was beating double time.

"Here's the deal," Joe said, his tone menacing. But his arms were down and his hands loose at his side. "Let her go and I don't beat the shit out of you."

Vicki shivered. She'd never heard Joe's voice so cold. But sudden warmth filled her as well. He wouldn't let Derek hurt her.

"You got an army with you?" Derek sneered, gesturing at the empty dock.

"Don't need one." Joe's strong voice kept her from falling completely apart. "You've got two seconds to let her go."

"Oh, like I'm scared. Isn't the new lover trying to play tough?"

"You don't want to find out how tough I am." Joe moved toward them.

Vicki squeezed her eyes shut against the pain radiating from her scalp when Derek tightened his hold. Then the pressure was gone, and a hand shoved her hard in the back and sent her flying. She opened her eyes to see Joe as he caught her, holding her against his body.

"Are you okay?" His gaze swept over her from head to toe.

"I'm better. You're here." She laid her icy palm on his forearm.

"So you like having a slut in your bed, do you?" Derek's voice dripped with derision. "Is he better than the last one? The one I scared away with a single phone call after he kissed you?"

Joe's muscles tensed. Beneath his hands, Vicki trembled.

"Let's get out of here," she said.

"Yeah, run away, little mouse. You're good at running, but you can't run forever. I'll find you, and then I'll settle the score. Boyfriend here can't protect you. I own you."

Derek was deranged, Joe realized. And it made him even more dangerous. He started to shift Vicki behind him when her spine stiffened.

"I'm not running, Derek." Her chin came up. Joe hadn't thought he could love her more than he already did, but he was wrong. She wasn't going to hide, not any more. "I tried it your way. It didn't work. The police are aware of you stalking me."

Derek laughed. "You've got nothing on me, little mouse."

"I have every letter, every message, every sick gift, and there's the box of black roses. I'm sure the police will find out who you bribed to deliver them and the note to me here at the hotel. Stalking is against the law, and so is assault. It's time for the law to be involved."

"You little bitch." Derek took a step forward, his fists clenched, rage blazing from his gaze.

Joe started to push Vicki behind him. "No, Joe." She placed a hand on his arm. Keeping one eye on Derek, he glanced down at her. "He's not worth it," she murmured, waving her arm and dismissing Derek as if he were a fly annoying her.

"No, he isn't." He ran a finger down her cool, pale cheek. Derek shifted. "But you are." Pivoting, Joe threw his punch before Derek could react. His knuckles stung after they made contact with the man's jaw, and he grinned with satisfaction when Derek fell on his ass.

Hotel security arrived on the scene, then right behind them the police.

Ignoring Derek's accusations that he was hit without provocation, Joe slipped his arm around Vicki's waist and maneuvered them away from the crowd. A heavyset police officer glared at them. "We'll be right over there, Officer." Joe gestured with his chin toward the bench sitting against the wall.

"Thank you, sir. We'll need statements from you both."

IT WAS MORE than two hours later before they made their way

back to their hotel room.

Derek was in police custody with not only the letter and flowers, but statements from the hotel employees he'd impersonated in order to deliver them. Management had also made complaints to the police about Derek hanging around the hotel bothering guests. He was no longer an issue. Vicki sighed as relief filled her. Derek was gone for good.

Once inside their room, Joe drew her into his arms and kissed her. Softly, gently, his lips caressed hers until he lifted his head and gazed down into her eyes. "I love you."

Vicki's heart stopped. He loved her? When did this happen?

"I know you're not ready for this," he continued. "But I'm not going to let another day go by without saying it. I love you and I want to marry you. I'll wait until you're ready, no matter when it is, but I wanted you to know."

She couldn't talk. Tears blocked her throat, and her arms tightened around his neck. "I … "

"Shhh." Joe pulled her against his chest as he ran his palms in circles over her back. "You don't have to say anything. After everything you've been through today, I couldn't keep it in any longer. I was so afraid for you."

Tilting her head, Vicki gazed up into his blue eyes and cleared her throat. "I love you, too."

Several seconds passed before the words sank in, then his eyes lit and he gave a yell before crushing her lips with his. "You know this means I'm never letting you go," he said when he broke the kiss.

"I wouldn't want it any other way. You belong to me, Joe Bradshaw." This was a different kind of possession, one of love, not control.

"I am your willing servant." He laughed as he lay her on the bed. "Tonight, my love, is all for you. Your wish is my command.

Anything your heart desires, it can have."

She opened her arms to him and smiled. "All I want is you."

ACKNOWLEDGMENTS

Thanks to my wonderful critique group, Nia, Isabel and Chandra, who help me brainstorm and kick me in the pants when I need it.

ABOUT THE AUTHOR

Marie Tuhart lives in the Pacific Northwest and can't remember a time when she didn't have a book in her hands. When she isn't reading or writing, Marie loves to spend time in bookstores and traveling. Marie's muse is her toy poodle, Penny, who lets Marie know when she's been working too long.

Find her online:

www.marietuhart.com
Facebook: facebook.com/Marie-Tuhart
Twitter: twitter.com/marietuhart
Pinterest: pinterest.com/marietuhart
Goodreads:goodreads.com/author/show/4190063.Marie_Tuhart

www.ingramcontent.com/pod-product-compliance
Lightning Source LLC
Chambersburg PA
CBHW050536190726
48284CB00003B/1091